Sew HAUTE

SNITCHES GET STITCHES

KAT ADDAMS

PLEASE BE ADVISED:

While this book is comedy, it contains a slight underlying theme of recognizing domestic abuse that might be sensitive to some readers.

Are you or someone you know experiencing abuse? Please get help today.

One

MADISON

I often heard that all it took was one person to change the course of someone's life. I'd never believed that crap until my best friend, Hailey, met her soul mate and gave up her entire inheritance to run off with a guy she barely knew. I would never understand it. Men before me? Yeah, right. I blazed my own path and walked my own runway.

My designer life would never change for anyone—not even if that particular someone wore a tailored Armani suit and talked with a sexy British accent. No one could con me into giving up my lifestyle for love. That divergence from a life plan didn't happen to women like me. I could see the forest for the trees, and I wasn't even an outdoorsy person. I was a boss babe—in total control of myself and untouchable to the drama that came with relationships. That was why my new man, Jeff, who was entirely independent on his own, complemented me so well.

I smirked, thinking of my bright future while dabbing at my forehead with a stiff, gym-provided towel. Spin class was the only time I allowed myself to let my thoughts loose, and these days leading up to finals and graduation, I needed to let them loose often. Forks University Fashion Academy had proven more stressful and exhausting than I could have ever imagined. And this year, I didn't have Hailey to vent to anymore. She'd traded mimosas and brunch for clovers and barns. To say I was shocked that she had abandoned me for a West Coast life filled with cows, chickens, and elk was an understatement. I hadn't even known what an elk was until she posted on her social media a photo of two horned beasts going at it in her backyard with the caption, *Vixen and Blixen*.

I'd never seen anything like a real-life reindeer before. But then again, I'd never made it off of Santa's naughty list either. That old bowl of Jell-O was much more apt to stop by my friend Cheri's room. She had a thing for graying sugar daddies. But I much preferred someone I could relate to—men in their early twenties with a future of fresh possibilities ahead of them. And swimming in money? No way. I didn't *need* any man's money. I'd worked tirelessly for years, building my fashion empire one stitch at a time. Money wasn't an issue. That wasn't to say I would date a lazy bum either.

The only characteristics I required in a man were complete independence and the entrepreneurial push-and-shove business attitude that turned me on—whether that brought him in money or not, I didn't care. I needed an alpha male who wasn't afraid to go after what he wanted—me. I'd admit, I was a bit intimidating. Any man who could handle me was immediately worth a date or three. My no-bullshit approach to life had scared away plenty of people, alpha men especially. But it had also brought me good business sense. I wasn't afraid to say no, and even better, I wasn't scared to say yes. I took calculated risks and excelled at reading the market, and my brand would one day be as iconic as the yellowing bottle of Chanel No. 5 on my grandmother's mirrored vanity.

I draped the scratchy towel around my neck and pushed the swinging door open to the locker room, dragging myself inside. A blast of cold air hit me in the face as I dialed my code in the padlock and swung open the locker. I stood frozen, catching my breath and admiring the beautiful piece of art that hung on the hook in the back—my Joanna James gym bag. I'd snagged one of the first editions on preorder six months ago. Although the ice-white material was a stupid choice for a bag used for dirty clothes, it drew attention to my matching hair—particularly Jeff's attention.

He was the reason I'd begun taking spin class in the first place.

A few weeks ago, I'd caught a glimpse of him strutting across the gym as if he owned it.

Jeff easily towered over the other men by a full six inches. His thin, sleeveless shirt clung to his chest, revealing deep, muscular ridges that begged to be touched. He stood in front of the mirror and curled a dumbbell in his fist, grunting with each lift. His gaze was focused on the bulging of his veins each time he flexed until he paused long enough to notice something equally as sexy as his biceps—me.

I matched his air of confidence with a few deep squats, pushing my apple bottom out and down while he openly watched. He reached for a water bottle, taking a long, slow drink before wiping his arm across his mouth and turning to leave.

The next time I saw him in the gym, he caught my gaze and winked before disappearing into a dark room. Naturally, I followed, thinking he was sending me some type of signal. But after I opened the door to a room full of bikes, I realized I had been sorely mistaken.

But pride was an issue for me. Instead of leaving like a dumbass, I straightened my spine and walked toward a bike situated in between two older women a row ahead of him. I had never taken a spin class in my life. My coordination for outdoorsy stuff, like biking, was the same as my coordination for other things outside of my element, like budgeting. It was nonexistent.

I made it ten minutes into the class before realizing that I needed special shoes to clip into the bike pedals. While the other people around me stood up during an incredibly fast-paced beat, I slipped off, crashed headfirst into the handlebar, and landed with my butt in the air, straddling the seat and fumbling for footing. The instructor immediately rushed to my side, lifting me back into position.

Above the music, she yelled in my ear about the importance of proper footwear and rushed off to grab a hideous pair of shoes. I cringed, sliding my feet inside the damp material that smelled ripe with mold and probably some geezer's toenail fungus. But as I'd said, pride was an issue for me. I snapped into the pedals and rode until well after the class finished. By the time I gathered enough courage to look up from the meter on my bike, everyone had left the room, and the sexy beast who lurked the gym was gone.

I picked up my ego and marched toward the locker room, gathering my bag to leave the gym ASAP.

But before I made it to the parking lot, a husky voice called out behind me, "Are you all right? Did you hurt yourself back there?"

I paused, swiveling on my heels. The sexy gym beast stood only a few feet from me. His lips curled upward into a wide grin.

"I'm fine," I offered, slinging my bag over my shoulder.

He rubbed his beardless jaw and nodded before looking away. His boyish features softened.

"How about a mimosa then? You know, I hear vitamin C can help a bruised butt, and alcohol can help a bruised ego." His gaze returned to mine.

I squinted my eyes and situated my bag across my body. The belt strap dug tight into my rib cage.

"Let's go then," I said.

He took a step toward me and extended his hand. "Great! I know just the place. I'm Jeff, by the way."

"I'm Madison." I gave him my best firm handshake.

My mother had taught me that when I introduced myself to anyone, I'd better straighten my posture and give off confidence even if it was fake. Lucky for her, her daughter wasn't fake at all. I'd always been true to my dramatic self.

"Madison, your bag matches your hair. I don't know if you intended that but well played. You're the most beautiful thing I've seen in this gym!"

A rush of heat had built between my legs, and the rest was history. We'd been fucking ever since.

I rummaged through my bag and searched for my phone. Jeff had had an early morning meeting with his tech firm, so our usual spin date was off the table. But he'd promised to schedule some time later today for catching up—and by catching up, I meant, more sex. Since our second—*who am I kidding*—first date, we couldn't keep our hands off of each other.

Besides my man's massively broad shoulders, meaty biceps, washboard abs, and chiseled jawline, his dominating attitude in bed sealed the deal for me. That man had taken me to new heights between the sheets. For once in my life, I didn't have to think of anything because Jeff took over total control. He chewed me up and spat me out—and I fucking loved it.

I unlocked my phone and scrolled through my texts, ignoring the messages from my mother.

> *Jeff: You know that thing we want to do before all the feels hit? I found someone to check that fantasy off the list.*

A faint burning sensation crept across my cheeks. I glanced behind me at the empty room and backed myself into a corner before answering.

> *Me: Guy? Girl?*
>
> *Jeff: Guy.*
>
> *Me: And you trust him?*

Jeff: He's an old friend. We don't talk much anymore. But I bumped into him last night while he was on the prowl. His words, not mine. He wouldn't stop talking about sex and women. I put some feelers out and casually dropped hints about my kinky new girlfriend. And how you wanted to do some exploring before things got serious.

I took the towel from around my neck and scrubbed my face with the rough cloth.

Me: When?

Jeff: Tonight. My place at 8.

I stumbled back into the wall, sliding down onto my bottom.

Me: I'll be there.

I set my phone down and took a deep breath. I'd come close to having two men at once not long ago. I'd made out with twins and rolled around in bed with a couple of frat boys. But I never actually did much other than kissing and touching. Surprisingly, my wild side had boundaries. Until I met Jeff anyway. He allowed me to explore in a way I felt safe. Just last week, he'd popped a ball gag between my lips, and I'd never been more excited to shut my mouth.

Of course, I hadn't told my BFFs, Hailey and Cheri, about my kink. I preferred to keep my boss-babe persona and tough exterior in public, but behind closed doors, I liked to give up the reins and put control in someone else's hands. Any sign of weakness was an enemy of mine.

I picked myself up off the floor and grabbed my bag, shuffling to the sink and checking my reflection in the mirror. My skin sparkled with a dewy glow, and my eyes shone bright underneath a row of thick mink lashes. I smiled, swiped a rosy shade of gloss across my lips, and held my phone out. I quickly snapped a selfie and hashtagged *strong women*, uploading it to my handful of social media accounts and hoping my legend lived on after my slutty threesome tonight.

"You're going to do what?" Cheri gasped, tossing a crystal dildo on her feathered bed.

"Don't get all judgy with me! You're prepping for your next cam show, for fuck's sake! It's not like you haven't done some wild shit before. I'm sure you've taken two at once ..." I sat up in her desk chair and tapped the blinding halogen spotlight pointed at her "stage."

"Women," she sighed. "My audience prefers that. They aren't into gang bangs or threesomes with two men. They either want me solo, to themselves, or with another lady."

"Huh. I've never experimented with a woman. What's that like?" I glanced at the camera set up on her laptop and moved away from its lens.

"It's like screwing someone who knows every single button to push on you without being told. They're gentle, but they also know when to be firm. They read signals like no man can. Plus, it's kind of fun, playing with boobs." She walked to her dresser mirror and began to tie her hair into pigtails.

"I don't know. I'm not saying I wouldn't, but ... I think I'd prefer a pair of dicks to a pair of boobs. Guess I'll find out tonight. I'm so damn nervous." I rubbed the back of my neck while watching her effortlessly change into her character, Lola Spanx.

Cheri had been a cam girl for the last two years, running her Lola Spanx brand. Last year, things had really taken off when she found her sugar-daddy niche.

She oozed innocence and playfulness. I, on the other hand, oozed a resting bitch face.

"Don't be nervous. You're going to live out every woman's fantasy. I want to fuck a basketball team myself, but I'd settle for two hotties. Who's the other guy anyway? I pity any man who has to measure up to Jeff. He looks like he could rip you in two."

She checked the time on her phone and shimmied out of her robe, letting it fall to the floor. A matching set of pale pink lacy lingerie hugged her hourglass curves. I recognized the overpriced brand. Even I would hesitate before making such a purchase.

"I'm not sure. An old friend of his, he said." I leaned forward in my chair and picked her silky robe off the floor before draping it across her desk and checking the label— Versace. Perhaps being a cam girl and playing with boobs had its perks.

"You're going to fuck someone you don't know? Now, that's too far!" Cheri put her hands on her hips and stared a hole through me.

"I trust Jeff."

"You barely know him!"

"I mean, I trust his judgment. He wouldn't just pick some guy off the street!"

"Still … you barely know him! And the other guy is a total stranger!"

"It's not like I haven't had a one-night stand before! Same thing. I'll be safe."

"Okay. What if you get pregnant or an STD? Earth to Madison. What has this man done to you? You're usually smarter. He could be a serial killer!" Cheri's voice rose to an alarming pitch.

"He won't be a serial killer! Or get me pregnant. Don't you know me? Babies are never in my future! I'm careful about that. I have protection." I threw my hands in the air and leaned back in her desk chair, groaning.

"Fine! What if he's ugly?" She shifted her feet and smirked.

"When the lights are off, a dick is a dick."

"Fuck! You're nastier than me. You sure you don't want to sit in on this? I've got an entire group of sugar daddies logging in." She nodded at the laptop. Sure enough, username after username was popping into her private chat.

"I'm not that nasty! Besides, I doubt I'll ever get the chance to do this again. Not with Jeff anyway. We're doing all the fun stuff before one of us catches the feels and gets jealous." I rose from the chair and stretched before making my way to her door. The last thing I wanted to watch was my best friend fiddling her diddle for a bunch of older men.

"Smart. You think you'll fall for him?" She pulled a long pink wand from her nightstand and set it on the bed. It instantly buzzed in sync with the dings coming from her laptop.

"Not now! But I think I could eventually. He's pretty much everything."

"Madison Sheffield, falling in love. That's something I never thought I'd see. I pictured you married to your work for life."

"Oh, that too. I'll be a two-timing whore with my brand and my man. Work is always going to be my true love. Maybe Jeff can be my side bitch. And maybe this other guy can be my side bitch-bitch. I think that's how it would work. Hell, send me your basketball team. I can find something for each one of them to do. Sexual or not."

"Living the dream." She laughed, walking toward her laptop. Her fingers flew across the keyboard.

"At least for tonight." I turned the knob on her door and slid out, shutting it behind me.

The sorority house was quiet from its usual low hum of constant chatter. My Beta Alpha Delta, or BAD, sisters took their work seriously. Finals week in the BAD house meant lots of caffeine, hormonal breakdowns, a handful of panic attacks, and unhealthy doses of stimulants. All of my sisters were on edge, but none had the weight of graduation on their shoulders, as I did. In just a week, I'd retire from sorority life and embark on a new journey into adulthood. I needed to go out with a bang—literally.

I made my way down the hallway and into my room to shower and dress. A night like tonight called for the sluttiest lingerie I had. Although I'd spent most of the semester in the fashion studio, designing my gym gear, I had secretly been making something more scandalous as a hobby. I'd designed the perfect piece for tonight, complete with lots of leather straps and chains to hook up and hang on to.

Long gone were my days of silk and fur-trimmed robes. These days, I much preferred a wild alter ego. I'd told myself it was a phase, and after the stress of graduation, maybe I would get back to normal. But I wasn't sure I wanted to get back to my normal. I liked letting go—just a little.

I arrived at Jeff's house early. I needed to set up and prepare myself for whatever would happen tonight, and that meant I needed his reassurance, a stiff drink, and about twenty minutes to change into my strappy lingerie. Whoever this third wheel was, he needed to at least know that I wasn't some cheap thrill. I came manicured, polished, primped, and primed, and he had better be too.

Jeff was always well dressed and well groomed. In his role as the boss of his tech firm, he always impressed. His home was immaculate, thanks to his two housekeepers. His car, a luxurious Alfa Romeo, still gave off the new-car smell even though he'd had it for two years. And best of all, his body was top-notch. Did I mention his chiseled abs?

The first time I'd stayed over at his place, he'd poured a bottle of champagne, flicked an app on his phone to turn on mood lights, and told his home robot-device thing to play smooth jazz. I was tech-savvy, but being in Jeff's house had felt like I'd landed on another planet. The man was very obviously a genius and very obviously successful at it. Once, when he'd taken me to dinner, he had made friends with the chef and taken on a consulting project for the restaurant, all over the course of two hours.

It hadn't been a surprise to me when he texted about the third guy. Jeff could talk anyone into anything. He charmed the pants off of me and plenty of others. Tonight, the poor second dick had big pants to fill, standing next to Jeff. Even I, Madison freaking Sheffield, sometimes felt unseen next to my man. There were times when we went out, and all eyes were focused on him instead of my latest Gucci purchase. I had mixed feelings about all that and zero time to figure them out.

"Madison?" Jeff called through his bathroom door.

I wound the leather straps around my breasts before opening the door.

"Sorry it's taking me so long."

"Fuck," he said, taking a step back and licking his lips. "I don't know if I can hold out much longer with you wearing that. Come here!"

He grabbed me by the waist and pulled me into him, pressing his mouth on mine. I could already taste the whiskey on his breath.

"Uh-uh!" I laughed, pushing him away. His rigid muscles flexed under my touch. "You have to save some for the other guy."

"Says who?" he growled.

"You're the one who set this up. Are you having second thoughts about sharing?" I asked.

"No." He blew out a breath. "Not really. It's just … my friend is your type."

"I have a type?"

"Of course." He leaned into the mirror and brushed a strand of hair from his eyes, turning his jawline at different angles and checking himself out.

"What's my type?"

"Me." He smiled, dropping his gaze from himself and back to me.

"Ah. So, he's hot, motivated, successful, and a total beefcake," I said.

"Bingo."

"And you're worried I'm going to run off with this twin of yours?" I pulled a sultry shade of lipstick out of my bag and swiped it across my lips.

The thought of two muscular meatheads chewing on me sent a tingle straight to my clit, but I tried to give him my best poker face to play my excitement down. I didn't want to hurt Jeff's ego. Because if the stiletto were on the other foot, someone would suffer my wrath.

"Maybe." He put his bulging arms around me and nuzzled my neck.

I caught a whiff of his intoxicating cologne; it was expensive and Italian. I couldn't even pronounce the name when he told me the brand. And I knew my designers—in fashion, fragrance, and all things luxury.

"Mmhmm. Am I growing on you?" I teased, turning to face him.

He looked down at me with steely-gray eyes, the color of sharkskin.

"Like a rare flower." He tucked my hair behind my ear and kissed my brow.

"Charming." I pressed my lips into a thin line, fighting off the urge to feel. I didn't have time for that.

All I needed was to let loose tonight and de-stress before my finals, so I could finally graduate, open my boutique, and do some adulting like a boss babe. Nothing would get in the way of that—not even two gorgeous men spit-roasting me like a juicy piece of meat.

I cleared my throat. "Ready to tie me up?"

"As ready as I'll ever be." He turned to leave and headed toward the bedroom, muttering something into his phone about heavy metal music.

The speakers in his room began to blare a wicked beat that felt downright sinful.

I took a deep breath and followed him. His bubble butt peeked over the top of his low-slung slacks. His squat record at the gym was more than impressive, and it showed.

"On the edge of the bed," he commanded, tipping his chin toward the platform mattress.

I shuffled my feet toward the bed, resisting the urge to skip. Again, I didn't want to hurt his ego. But tonight was a fantasy I'd toyed with for ages. Who wouldn't want multiple men fawning over them?

He lit a few candles and turned off the lights before reaching for a rope from his nightstand.

"Remember," he said, jerking my wrists behind my back and tying them up in quick, rough movements, and the rope cut into my skin, burning it with each knot he tied, "you're mine."

I swallowed hard, stuck my nose in the air, and nodded.

The fuck I am, said that annoying voice in my head that always wanted to fight back. This *loss of control* thing didn't suit my conscience well even if it was only for a night.

"I'm yours," I said through clenched teeth before he buckled the ball gag around my head.

"Good girl. I think I hear him knocking. I'll be back. Do you need anything before I bring him in?" He smoothed my hair down my shoulders and stood back, studying me.

I shook my head. Heat coursed through my veins the second he left the room and shut the door.

What if this new guy is ugly?

What if he's a psycho?

What if he's not planning on using a condom? How can I tell him with this damn gag in my mouth?

What if he thinks I'm ugly?

Yeah, right.

My thoughts began to run wild, skyrocketing my pulse.

In just a few short moments, I'd be in the arms of not one, but two men. They would pass me around like a toy, using me for their pleasure while giving me mine. I wondered if there was a chance that they'd both fuck my pussy at the same time, sliding themselves into my tight, little hole and making me feel full. My clit began to tingle, aching to be touched as I imagined the man's tongue between my legs while Jeff slid his dick down my throat. My skin prickled, stiffening my nipples.

I squirmed on the edge of the bed, ready to take them both and prove to them just how tough this dainty, little body could be. The faint sound of footsteps in the hallway echoed above the music. Shadows stepped into the light from underneath the bedroom door. My heartbeat spiked, thumping hard through my chest.

I sat up tall, straightening my spine. Jeff opened the door and stepped aside, letting our third wheel into his bedroom. I squinted, unsure of if my eyes were playing tricks on me or not. But after he opened his loud mouth and said my name, I knew the joke was on me. Preston Lancaster, my brother's cocky best friend and my worst enemy, stood, towering over my very naked—and very vulnerable—body.

I looked from Jeff to Preston and back again, searching their eyes for some kind of hint that would tell me this was a prank. But Jeff looked as surprised as I did. This bullshit rendezvous must have been Karma for the shenanigans I'd pulled on Preston and his fraternity brothers at the Delta Iota Kappa house—or DIK-heads, as I liked to call them.

Preston took a step toward me, unbuttoning his shirt. I didn't care that he was as hot as Jeff or that the bulge in his pants was like a python ready to strike. Preston thought he could win this fight because of my unfortunate position. But I'd never give him that. He would bow to me, like the rest of them.

This wasn't just sex. This was war.

PRESTON

My hands grew slick the moment I knocked on Jeff's front door. I'd never fucked both a man and woman at the same time because having my balls close enough to kiss another man's sack during a muffin stuffin' skeezed me the hell out. Sure, I'd fucked plenty of women at the same time. Last summer, I'd scored three on my dick at once. But that was the extent of multiples in my bed. Imagining a man between my sheets and stealing attention from my date was a no-go.

But this chick my old friend Jeff had kept bragging about already had me ready to tag-team her with a night she would never forget. He told me she liked to lose control. And me? I very much wanted to be in control. When he hinted at her fantasy of being banged by two meaty jocks at once, I readily volunteered as tribute. I'd long ago accepted the brutal truth that I liked women to crumple in my hands.

"Come in." Jeff opened the door and let me pass.

He slightly towered over me, but when it came down to it, his girl would have more trouble peering over my broad shoulders than his.

"Thanks." I dipped my head and stepped inside.

A deep, woodsy musk drifted through the air, like he'd recently come in from chopping wood or hunting buffalo. I scanned the living room for mounted animal heads but only saw works of art and a surprisingly stylish yet masculine interior.

"Can I offer you a drink before we get started?" He strolled to a drink cart and clinked two ice cubes into a glass before pouring from a bottle of whiskey.

I knew the bottle from across the room. It was the same Irish whiskey my dad bought himself every Christmas. The price on one bottle could pay for an entire semester at FU, and this dude poured me a double.

"Started? Is she already here?" I asked, reaching for the glass. My heart pounded in my chest. I took a sip of the whiskey and grunted. The alcohol slowly burned throughout my chest, dulling my anxiety.

"She's ready when we are. I set her up how she likes in the bedroom." He poured himself a glass and took a swig.

"How does she like it?"

"To be used."

"Come again?" I blinked.

"She's wild. She likes to be a fuck toy. Dominated. Thrown on the bed and fucked senseless. She likes to be tied up and gagged. I'm sure a man like you knows this type. Hell, it's practically all of the women I've been with. They all want to let go in bed. It's their natural instinct. Women need to be controlled." He smirked.

He wore the same smug look on his face that he'd had the day he left the DIK house. He'd only been a member for two months before thinking he was better than his brothers and quitting the fraternity. We'd parted ways shortly after that.

I weighed his words before answering. His face was arrogant and punchable. I'd always had a gut feeling from Jeff that there was more to him below the surface. But besides his pretentious attitude, I could never figure him out. To me and everyone else, he was extremely charismatic, clever, and successful. He was just like me.

"What're the rules? We've not really talked much about this. It was kind of sudden."

"Are you backing out?" He raised a perfectly shaped eyebrow.

"Of course not." I cleared my throat. "I don't want to step on any toes. She's your girlfriend, and I'm fucking her. I don't want any drama."

He set his glass on a stone coaster etched with a golden *J* and curled his lips into a smile.

"She's not my girlfriend. Not yet anyway. We've only been dating for two months. We're in that *new relationship energy* phase with zero feelings. So, while the getting is good, we're getting. You just so happened to be at the right place at the right time. And I know her type. I want to make her happy. She's good for me. There aren't any rules."

"Really?" I squinted over my glass, downing the rest of the whiskey entirely in one big gulp.

"Really."

"Well, I have one." I swirled the ice cubes before setting my drink down.

"What?"

"You have to stay away from my dick and balls. And my ass. I'm a ladies' man."

"I wouldn't touch your dick if your cum shot out gold." He laughed.

"Good." I grinned. "Now, let's go play with your new toy."

He turned to leave, motioning for me to follow.

We walked down a dark, wood-paneled hall and toward a door situated between two flickering sconces. The low hum of heavy metal music rang out from under it. I didn't know if I was about to enter a bedroom or a dungeon.

"As I said, she likes it wild. Don't say I didn't warn you." He opened the door and led me inside a room blazing with the light of a dozen candles.

But I didn't need any light to see the familiar gleam of stark white hair tumbling down her shoulders. Madison Sheffield glowed with an ethereal beauty that her bratty personality didn't deserve. My best friend's little sister and my number one enemy sat at the foot of the bed with her hands tied behind her. She wore black leather straps, cutting into her petite, little body. Her plump lips were wrapped tight around a ball gag. For once, she couldn't speak.

My voice caught in my throat before I gained my composure and realized I could finally pay her back for all the shit she'd given me over the years.

"Madison," I sneered, drawing near her and unbuttoning my shirt.

She squirmed against her restraints, looking to Jeff and me and back again with wide eyes.

"Do you two know each other?" Jeff asked, pausing before stepping out of his pants and letting them fall to the floor.

"Kind of." I studied Madison's perfectly sculpted breasts.

I remembered when she'd had the surgery to get them done years ago. I made fun of her then too. But I'd accidentally bumped across her several times in the weeks following, just to brush up against them and see if they felt as good as they looked.

She mumbled something into the gag as her eyes sparked with rage.

"I'm sorry, darling. I can't hear you. But did I say that you could speak?" Jeff reached across the bed and grabbed a long, narrow whip.

He raised it in the air and cracked it sideways, smacking it against her hip. She winced.

My blood boiled, echoing my pulse back to me in my ears. I clenched my fists at my sides.

She lifted her gaze to mine, peeking out from under a row of thick lashes.

"Is this going to be a problem?" Jeff asked, stroking the back of Madison's head.

I bit my lip and waited on her response. The last thing I would do to my best friend was fuck his little sister without her consent. No matter how bad she deserved for me to rip her in two.

She narrowed her eyes at me and shook her head.

I let out a breath I hadn't even known I was holding.

"Good girl." Jeff took the whip and trailed it along her chest.

Her nipples stiffened into two pink buds I ached to feel against my tongue.

My cock grew thick against my thigh.

Jeff tossed the whip on his bed and crawled behind her, sitting on his knees. He rested his hands on her shoulders. "Don't be shy, Preston."

Madison smirked, daring me.

I swallowed hard and dropped my boxers, letting my dick spring up at full mast. Her high-perched breasts rose as she took a deep breath and studied my girth. As far as I was concerned, it was my best asset.

Jeff tangled his fingers in her hair and forced her head to the side, exposing her neck. He dragged his lips down the soft flesh of her shoulder, biting her in quick nibbles. But her gaze never left mine. She wiggled her hips and moaned before spreading her legs wide and showing me her silken, smooth pink slit.

I took two steps and grabbed her between the legs, rubbing my thumb down her clit and shoving it inside her pussy. She was already dripping. Her lips curled around the ball gag.

"You like that, don't ya?" I pulled my thumb out and pushed two fingers inside of her.

She scrunched her brows together and sneered.

Jeff moved around her body, taking her breast in his mouth. She arched her back and moaned, grinding her hips into my fingers as he sucked her nipple. I gripped my cock in my palm and gave it a few hard tugs while I finger-fucked her pussy. She watched me until he dragged his mouth from her chest and stood up slowly.

"I think it's time to remove this gag. Don't you, baby? There's a better use for that mouth." Jeff unhooked the ball gag from the back of her head and tossed it aside.

I pulled my fingers away from her and stepped back, preparing myself for a verbal assault.

But Madison didn't say a word. Instead, she wrapped a hand around my cock and pulled me close, viciously spitting on the tip of my dick before shoving it in her mouth. I moaned, gathered her hair in my fists, and held her head steady as I eased myself down her throat. Her body lurched as she gagged. I pulled back, letting her catch her breath before I did it again. I picked up my pace and held her down on my cock as she spread her legs and fought against me.

Jeff ran his hands down her hair and pulled her off before nudging me to the side of the bed. Standing in front of her, he shoved her on his dick. She looked up at him. Her eyes watered as she struggled to breathe. A rush of heat shot through me as I watched her take his entire cock down her throat. Her high, exotic cheekbones rose as she opened her mouth wide.

He grunted before pulling her head away and stepping back. He turned her head to face me and pushed her back onto me.

"That's it. Take his cock." He bobbed her head down my shaft.

I dropped my head back and slid my eyes shut. When I opened them again, Jeff was squatting between her legs, licking her velvet pussy. I inched away, putting distance in between me and Jeff so that his smug face wasn't anywhere near my junk. Madison leaned back on the bed, never letting go of my cock.

"Fuck," she moaned. "Untie me. Un-fucking-tie me." Her eyes cut to mine. She rolled on her side toward me, showing me her wrists behind her.

I fumbled with the rope while she bucked against Jeff's face. She craned her neck closer to me and caught my balls with her tongue as I leaned over her.

I groaned, untied her, and pushed her back flat on the bed. But before I could shove her douche-bag boyfriend out of the way and bury myself into her wet pussy, she grabbed my hips and stopped me. Madison turned her attention back to my cock, opened her mouth wide, and showed me her tongue. She wanted more. I reached out, curling my fingers over her throat and squeezing. I slid my dick between her lips, fucking her reddening face again while bringing her past her own will. She struggled, wrestling me off and gasping for breath. I tried to step back further from the side of the bed so that I could let her breathe, but she grabbed my hips and shoved me back down her throat, sucking me in a series of gulps.

Fuck, she's destroying me.

I swayed before I tumbled over in horny, drunken delirium.

Jeff rose, slipping his hands underneath her and flipping her over onto her stomach. He grabbed her around the middle and pulled her to her knees. She immediately put me back in her mouth.

"Here," he said, tossing me a condom he'd grabbed from who knew where.

My mind was on Madison and her deep-throating my dick like a champ. Her bratty mouth was good for something.

I watched Jeff as he slipped a condom on and eased himself inside of her. Her eyes bulged as she let my dick fall out of her mouth. She turned her head and cried out, locking her eyes on his. He gripped her tiny waist and drove into her, nearly knocking her off her knees. I slid my fingers into her mouth, curling my palm around her chin and forcing her head back to me.

She glanced up at me for a second and bit down on my fingertips. Her eyes rolled back into her head as he pounded her hard.

What the fuck?

I stood, pumping my dick in my hand, maddened with need. I was losing in this fuck-off—and I didn't lose. Especially to Madison.

I dropped my hand from her mouth and grabbed the condom, sliding it on before I walked behind her.

"Tag, you're it," Jeff said.

He pulled out and made his way to her head. She let out a moan and stretched, putting her hips further into the air.

"You want this pussy, don't you, Preston? Just admit it. You always have."

I glanced at the ball gag before turning my attention back to her.

"I don't want your pussy. I'm fucking your ass." I slapped her hard across her ass cheek, leaving my red handprint on her sun-kissed skin.

She gasped. Jeff paused before exchanging grins with me. He opened his nightstand drawer and tossed me a bottle of lube.

"Think you can handle us both?" he asked, sliding underneath her. He gripped his dick and ran it up her slit back and forth before driving it inside of her.

She looked back at me, scrunching her brows together. A pleading look flashed briefly in her eyes as I positioned myself on the bed behind her, spreading her ass cheeks and pouring the lube down her crack.

"Heh. Can I? Can you two handle me?" She licked her lips, curling the bedsheets into her fists and breathing deep. A tinge of unsteadiness snuck in her voice, but I didn't care. If she said she wanted it, she wanted it.

I pushed the tip of my dick on her tight, little asshole, slowly easing my thickness inside of her. She flinched and sucked in a quick breath through her teeth. A tremor shook in her thighs as her muscles clenched down on my cock with an impressive grip.

"Relax," I said, lightly running my hand down her back. Her skin prickled under my touch.

She took another deep breath as I eased myself further inside, deliberately stretching her out until she took my entire cock.

"Oh fuck!" she cried, shivering.

I briefly made eye contact with Jeff, who didn't seem the least bit worried about her pain. I could feel his cock moving inside of her with each reckless thrust of his hips. He looked away before closing his eyes and hammering into her harder.

I paused, leaning down and circling her neck with my arm.

"Tell me if you want me to stop. You don't have to do this," I whispered in her ear.

She turned her face toward me. A faint shimmer of sweat glowed across her brow.

"Are you chickening out? Can't fuck me in the ass?" she whispered back. Her bratty attitude played across her grin.

I blew a breath out and squeezed her neck in the crook of my elbow while I slid my cock back and forth in her ass. I rose, spreading her firm ass cheeks in my palms. She turned her face toward me, locking on my eyes in a half-lidded gaze.

A flash of pain hid behind those eyes, but she mumbled, "Don't stop," and I was no quitter.

She bucked against our cocks, and we all three moved in a tense rhythm. It only took one of us to start a chain reaction. Once Jeff grunted and lifted his hips, Madison lost control. Her body shook underneath me as she spasmed on my dick. She cried out in a series of quick and loud gasps, like she felt a hell of pleasurable pain. I dug my fingertips into her hips and released myself inside her with one last deep push.

It wasn't until her body stopped trembling that I was able to gently take myself out, followed by Jeff. He quickly rolled out from under her and headed straight to a bathroom.

Madison fell to her side and caught my eye.

"If you ever tell anyone about this, I will royally fuck up your entire life," she said between ragged breaths.

"You aren't mad now, are ya?" I grinned.

I rolled over in bed and checked my phone on the nightstand. I had precisely twenty minutes before my first final began. Not that it mattered if I passed or failed that exam. My future was in the bag regardless. My family owned several local banks in Forks and the surrounding areas, which meant I would inherit them one day without doing much of anything. But after carelessly failing enough courses to set me back over a year, and disappointing my mom, I couldn't afford to repeat yet another year. I had to at least get up and do the work, or I would never leave FU.

I rubbed my eyes and squinted at the bright screen on my phone. My heart plummeted into my stomach when I noticed Seth, my best friend, had texted me several times in the middle of the night. If he knew I'd fucked his sister, that would be the end of my bromance with my boy.

> *Seth: I can't make it to town for Madison's graduation. I've got an important meeting for a big opportunity. I already spoke with Madison, and she told me work comes first. So, there are no hard feelings. But I'm headed out to the lake house after my meeting. Want to meet me there like old times?*

I let out a breath.

Seth: Oh, and I'm bringing someone, just FYI. That same woman I've been dating. Melanie. No pressure on you to find someone or anything. We can still do bro stuff.

Me: Yeah, I'll be there.

I sat up in bed and swallowed hard. Seth was my ride-or-die homey. As teenagers, we'd made a pact that we would become bachelors for life. We didn't want to be tied down to one woman when there was plenty for us to indulge. But these last few months, he'd been exclusively dating Melanie, and our pact was quickly crumbling. If Seth was bringing a date to the lake, I would need one too. And women during finals week were hard to come by. They were all too focused on their careers and futures to pay me much attention. Which meant I was left with scraps.

I mentally scanned my little black book while slipping into my clothes. Cheryl from class was an option, but she had the annoying habit of spitting when she talked. One time, after a blowie, we'd gone back downstairs to hang out. She excitedly made conversation with my fraternity brothers, showering them in my dick juice each time she sputtered out a laugh. I felt terrible that my boys were walking around, oblivious to my other boys on their faces. But I didn't feel bad enough to stop it. I'd let her run her mouth all night.

Besides, we were just casual, like every other woman I banged. I hadn't ever come close to settling down, and I didn't plan on it. There were too many Cheryls, Christinas, Megans, Sarahs, and Leslies in the world.

Oh, Leslie. I would call that nympho up in a heartbeat if I could. But the last time we'd fucked, her boyfriend had burst through the door right as I was pounding her from the back. I didn't know she wasn't single, but even if I had, I doubted I'd have cared. With an ass like that, who could resist?

Her boyfriend scurried off in a fit of tears, followed by her. I'd later learned Leslie had a sex addiction. So, I guessed you could say I was like a drug.

I flexed my pecs in the mirror and nodded before heading off to class. The disadvantage of fucking my way through the hotties of Forks was that there wasn't many left. The ones I hadn't fucked yet all wanted serious relationships or were becoming engaged, married, or turning lesbian before I had a chance to give them "The P."

Hell, even my casual side piece I'd had over the last few years, Amber, had distanced herself. She was exactly like me, except without a penis. She loved no-strings sex, didn't want anything to do with love, spent her nights in the gym, and could perform a mean keg stand. But I made the mistake of bringing her around my parents—not because I had feelings, but because I thought it would quiet my mom's nagging about me settling down. It didn't. After dinner number two with the parents, my mom had started talking about weddings, and Amber had vanished.

I couldn't blame her. I would have bailed out of that too. But my pickings were now slim in this town, which left me with the uggos and the crazies.

Madison.

The thought stopped me in my tracks.

I'd only bumped into her once following the night I spread her apart. She'd ducked her head and run away before I could shoot her my dimpled grin. But there was no forgetting what we had done. And as much as I hated to admit it, she had taken me and her boyfriend like a champ. For all her shit-talking, she backed it up. Literally—on my cock. The way I had torn her apart still played in my brain daily, nightly, and sometimes quickly between classes. I'd jerked off more times this week than I had in ages. I felt like I was twelve and just discovering my dick again.

I tried to get into my nerd zone and think about the psychology behind my naughty thoughts with my worst enemy. It had to be a mental thing. There was no way I was sexually attracted to Madison. Sure, she was hot as fuck. And if I didn't know her, I would have probably tried to sleep with her. But Madison was Madison. When we were younger, she had been the brattiest know-it-all—and still was. Countless times, she had ruined whatever nefarious activities Seth and I were up to.

Once, when Seth and I were in high school, we'd planned a senior prank. Our friend Dave owned a farm and graciously let us borrow a few hundred chickens. Seth and I rented two eighteen-wheeler trucks to haul chickens to school. We planned on letting them loose before anyone else arrived at school the next morning, but Madison busted us out to her mom, who in turn called my mom. Seth and I had to return the chickens to Dave and scrub the inside of the trucks all day. I'd had the scent of chicken shit stuck in my nose for days, all because Madison couldn't keep her mouth shut.

She was a rule-follower, a Goody Two-shoes, and a huge ass-kisser. I was not. I flew by the seat of my pants to the disappointment of only my mom. My dad understood. He had been a DIK fraternity member too. And once a DIK, always a DIK. Mischief and mayhem were practically in my blood.

But that didn't stop my mom from swinging the hammer. She easily had both my dad and me wrapped around her pinkie, and that was before she struggled with breast cancer. After her diagnosis and recovery, my party-hard lifestyle had been brought down a notch. But just a notch. For all my shenanigans, she still thought I was the perfect son.

But I couldn't settle down like my dad even if I found a woman as perfect as my mom. I knew she wanted a daughter-in-law and grandbabies, but I couldn't wreck my life. I had a world to see and women to bang before starting up the lame nine-to-five adulting.

So, I had done what any other man in my position would do. I'd bought a dog, Sanchez, and claimed him as the DIK mascot. Anytime my mom asked for an update on my love life, I'd send Sanchez to "Grandma's" house.

The last time I'd let my mom babysit Sanchez, he'd come back with a new collar, home-baked treats, and even a posh jacket. I kept my playboy lifestyle, my mom had a snuggle buddy, and DIK's dog was styling. Winning!

I didn't need a woman's love in my life to love my life. I was perfectly happy, partying and remaining a forever bachelor.

MADISON

The day before graduation, I'd spent the entire morning in the design studio, putting on a few final touches on my project before my end-of-year presentation to the board. I stretched my neck, arching my back and reaching toward the ceiling with a yawn. I'd recruited three BAD sisters to help me in my showcase. Each would wear a different style of my growing athletic brand, Minx. Although I needed to pass this final to reach my personal goal, I didn't need to for financial or business reasons. Minx had taken off after the Christmas charity fashion show. I already had contracts with four different local boutiques for my apparel.

I was an entrepreneur and my own boss. My fashion degree was bragging rights only, which I'd admit, I utilized those rights at every soiree or gala. My mother, Liza Sheffield, was a notorious sponsor for FU's fashion program. She'd cultivated the program to the success it was today—a step toward making Forks more fashion-forward and on-trend.

Liza was not only my mother, but also the biggest hurdle I had in my academic life. She was tougher on me than any other student. Day after day, she'd nag me about my studies, my marketing plans, my sketches. No child of hers would disgrace the name she'd built for herself. That was part of the reason why my brother had moved away from her drama. But I admired her for it.

My mom had balls of steel and an iron fist to match. She didn't bake cookies or put up Christmas decorations. We hired help for that. My mother wouldn't be caught dead in an apron. At times, I even questioned why she'd had kids. Goodness knows, our family wasn't very fond of them, me included. But I never faulted my mom for her lack of nurturing. She made up for it by teaching me how to dig my designer heels into the ground of a cruel, cruel world and viciously conquer it.

I kneaded my shoulder. The sisters would arrive any minute to change and walk to the stage with me, where I'd not only display my unique talent for design, but also my exceptional talent for winning.

Thanks, Mom!

"If it isn't little Miss Fashion Icon, creator of Minx, boss babe of Forks, and sexy vixen of my bedroom, Madison Sheffield!" Jeff stepped into the studio and clapped. His lips parted to reveal a row of perfectly straight and blindingly white teeth—freshly bleached. I knew. I did it often too.

"What're you doing here?" I shook out my hair, tucking a wild strand behind my ear.

His smile slipped. "What do you mean? I came to see you and wish you well. I thought you'd be happy. If you want me to go …" he said.

A wave of guilt washed over me. I tilted my head and adjusted my smile, mentally reminding myself of my *resting bitch face* curse.

"No. That's not what I meant! I was just surprised, is all. I'm a bit flustered with this final. No worries." I inched forward, standing on my toes to reach his lips.

His mouth twisted back into a grin. "Good. I like surprising you. Especially with this." He reached into the front pocket of his jacket and pulled out a tiny blue Tiffany box before handing it to me.

"Jeff! What did you get me?" I gasped, clasping the gift with shaky fingers.

"Go on. Open it."

I took the top off the box and peered inside. A small stiletto pendant made out of diamonds sat nestled in velvet.

"Oh my gosh! This is gorgeous!" I squealed, taking the necklace out. I pressed it to my collar and turned my back to Jeff, so he could help me with the clasp.

"I thought you might like it. I wanted to give you something for graduation before all your other suitors did." He laughed.

"Ha! Only one of those these days." I turned back around, throwing my arms around him and squeezing. "Thank you so much."

"Get a room," Cheri said, barging into the design studio with the other two models following on her heels.

"Yeah, yeah. We will. Later." I pulled myself away from Jeff and winked.

"I know you're busy. I only wanted to drop by and give you that and wish you well on your final presentation. I know how important it is. I'll see you tonight. Knock 'em dead!" He backed out of the room, waving good-bye to my sisters and me.

I pressed my hand to the hollow of my neck, feeling the cold diamonds under my fingertips.

"You'd better wipe that ridiculous grin off your face. You're scaring me." Cheri dropped her bag on the table.

I cleared my throat and pressed my lips into a thin line. "Right. On with the show!"

"Is your mom a judge?" one of the sisters, Sarah, asked.

"No. They have a stand-in. They didn't want it to be unfair, thankfully! She would've butchered me. But I got this—one small step into opening up my store. I want to see my brand in the big stores, on billboards, and flashing across Times Square."

"So, I can say I knew you when you weren't famous," Cheri said.

"Who said I'm not famous? Do you have any idea how many followers I have? Now, everyone, huddle for a selfie." I gathered the women around me and took a quick group photo, hashtagging *finals week*. The sooner I got this over with, the sooner I could get started on Minx full-time and give up college life for something much more glamorous. But first, I needed a break.

I planned to run off to our family's lake house for a few weeks this summer. It would be my first trip with a man. If Jeff could handle me after the first two weeks, I'd possibly consider making us official. But until then, my boyfriend was Minx. I adjusted my diamond necklace and took a deep breath.

"Are you nervous?" one of the younger recruits asked.

"Yes." I smiled. "But not about this."

I swept my portfolio in my arm and walked out the door to end my reign at FU.

"Mom, it's not a big deal!" I swatted her hand from my graduation cap as she tried to adjust it on my head.

"It most certainly is a big deal! Look, just because you have the Sheffield name and the Sheffield attitude, it doesn't give you a free pass in life. You need this degree. You're talented, but FU helped you get there. Humble yourself a bit." My mother situated my hair over my shoulders and stood back, studying my profile.

"Says the woman who showed up to my graduation in a diamond choker and Chanel suit." I craned my neck over the crowd, looking for Jeff.

He'd called to tell me his meeting had run late, but he should have been here by now.

"That mouth will be your downfall," she said.

"Ms. Sheffield!" Preston came up from behind me, hugging my mom. "I haven't seen you in ages! You look just as gorgeous as ever. I love the choker. Yeow!" He bit his knuckles.

My heart raced, pulsing loudly in my ears. The memory of his eyes on mine while he pounded away, mid–O face, shot to the front of my brain.

"Preston." She smiled. "Whenever you're around, there's bound to be trouble. Did you rig this graduation with a trailer of turkeys? I don't want feathers in my hair or bird shit on my boots."

"Not today, Ms. Sheffield. I'm just dropping by to wish Madison happy graduation. I promise. No mischief." He held his hands in the air.

I eyed him with a calculated expression. This was entirely out of character and completely unexpected. He was up to something.

"Really? That's awfully nice of you," Mom said.

"Yeah, well, I was in the area. Figured I'd *slide* right in real quick." Preston lifted his chin toward me.

"Thanks. I'm good. Appreciate it." I stuck my hip out and drew my brows together.

"You're welcome. You look perfect, by the way. I know how much detail and perfection means to you. You've always been so *anal*." Preston brushed an imaginary piece of dirt off my graduation gown.

"She gets it from me." My mom sighed.

I cringed, sucking in my breath.

"Does she?" Preston rubbed his chin between his thumb and index finger. His boyish grin dimpled.

I wanted to slap him.

"Good evening," said a voice over the loudspeaker, calling our attention. "Will everyone please begin to make your way to your seats? We will begin the commencement ceremony shortly."

"Better haul *ass* up there. You don't want to get left *behind*," Preston whispered.

"No worries. I've got a *tiny* bit of time," I whispered back in a harsh breath while holding out my thumb and finger an inch apart. "Jealous it's not you up there? Who fails freshman courses anyway? Guess I won this race."

Preston flinched.

"Madison, go. I'll be in the front." My mother tugged at my gown, pushing me toward the front of the auditorium. "It was good to see you, Preston! Tell your parents I said hi!"

She parted ways, running off to join her colleagues.

I whirled on my heels and stuck my nose in the air, dismissing him with a mere shrug of my shoulder. I pushed my way through the crowd. Jeff stood up ahead, waiting for me. I swallowed hard, hoping he didn't see the exchange between Preston and me.

"There's the graduate! So proud of you!" Jeff threw his arms around my waist, picking me up and spinning us.

I let out a sigh of relief.

"I'm so glad you're here," I said.

"I wouldn't have missed it for the world. Now, go get 'em, tiger!" He ushered me off toward the students nearby the stage. "I'll be right there." He nodded toward a row of seats nearby Cheri and a few of the BAD members.

I could recognize my sorority sisters easily. Their posh attire stood out, commanding attention. Today, they'd coordinated their outfits complete with classy hats that only they could pull off.

"I'd like to welcome you all to Forks University." The dean's voice rang out above the crowd as she situated herself at the podium.

I settled in my assigned seat and waited for what seemed like forever for them to call my name. I wasn't worried about walking across the stage and tripping or falling down the stairs. I was only nervous that Jeff would see Preston, and I would somehow have to explain my relationship with my brother's best friend and my worst enemy.

"Madison Sheffield!" a voice called.

I rose to my feet, brushing the thoughts of drama from my mind, and held my head high. My mother stood at the front of the stage, snapping pictures and smiling. My sisters stood up, cheering and holding signs plastered with my name in gold glitter. I walked across the stage amid a cheering crowd and a round of applause. An air horn blared from the back.

Preston.

He still stood where I'd left him. His lips parted in a goofy grin as he stuck his tongue out and gave me a thumbs-up and another toot of his air horn. I fought back a smile.

"Congratulations, Miss Sheffield," the dean said, handing me my diploma.

I paused for a few pictures while letting my gaze fall on Jeff. He sat with his face buried in his phone, completely unaware of me or his surroundings. I caught my smile before it slipped. I'd met my match. Work always came first.

The lake house was exactly how I remembered from my summers before college. Even though our family rarely vacationed there these days, it had been kept immaculate by our on-site keepers, Fred and Margaret. The husband-and-wife duo was unlike any couple I'd ever met. Instead of cordial greetings, they gave hugs. Instead of business small talk, they asked about our family and told us about theirs.

Instead of turning on the television or opening up a laptop, they sat and watched the sunset together, laughing.

I'd never seen an old couple so in love before. The only model relationships in my life centered around business or transactions. My mother sometimes married for money, and the man married her for her beauty and power. After things became stale, they'd part ways. But over the years, Margaret and Fred had seemed to grow closer, not apart. I'd often catch them dancing in the kitchen or cuddling by the firepit. Once, I'd even seen Fred grab a handful of Margaret's ass as they walked the wooded path down to their cottage.

Their love was a mystery to me. The sappiness made me uncomfortable but curious. I wondered how my life would have been different if I'd had parents like them. They were, in a sense, family to me—much like I'd expect grandparents to be if mine were still alive. Margaret had tried to teach me to cook but given up after I almost burned our kitchen down. Fred had tried to teach Seth to fish, but he'd also given up after Seth hooked his own mouth and ended up in the emergency room. They'd finally settled on loving us as we were—which, admittedly, was a lot to handle.

"Ah, this is the place where you spent your summers. It's beautiful." Jeff stepped out of the rental car and popped open the trunk.

I hopped out of the car and took a deep breath, filling my lungs with the familiar earthy scent of water and woods. "Yep. Our home away from home."

"I bet you have all kinds of stories to tell me. But I bet none involve getting dirty." He laughed before hoisting our luggage from the back of the car.

"Not *dirt under my nails* dirty. But plenty of the other." I walked toward him, looped my arms around his waist, and pulled him into me.

"I can only imagine." He cradled my head in his hands and tilted my chin up to him, kissing me gently—almost too gently and sweet for me.

I smiled and pulled away, busying myself with my bags. I'd brought my entire wardrobe, just in case I needed to go out to a fancy dinner or hike a trail through the forest.

Yeah, right.

I didn't hike or need to lose myself in the woods. Bugs and mud weren't my things. But that didn't mean I hadn't bought this season's hiking boots. If I ever needed to climb a mountain, I was prepared—fashionably, of course.

"Hey, why aren't you wearing the necklace I bought you?" His gaze dropped to my collar.

"Oh. Well, I was worried I'd lose it out here. Besides, it's too nice to bring to a lake house! You do know we'll be tanning out on the dock where the water is, right? It could get crusted with amoebas and whatever those little floaty things were I saw under a microscope in fifth-grade science class!" I shivered and picked up two of my bags before heading to the front door.

I blamed grade school for my hatred of all things wild. When we'd had to dissect a frog was when I suddenly became anti-nature. I took one look at the slimy creature spread open and ran to the restroom to hurl. From then on, I hadn't touched anything icky—save for the one time a man asked me to perform a prostate massage. I couldn't navigate inside of a frog's body, much less the guy's ass.

But I never backed down from a challenge. I'd twirled my finger up his poop chute until his legs shot up into the air and I hit the jackpot. After seeing how much power I could wield with that trick, it became the only loophole to my non-icky rule.

"What? Really? It's an everyday necklace. You looked stunning in it. I thought maybe you didn't like it." Jeff slowly followed behind me, weighed down with five of my bags and two of his.

"Don't be silly! I love it. I just didn't want to mess it up." I set my bags down and pushed the numbers on the keypad, unlocking the door.

Jeff's phone buzzed in his pocket.

"I've got to take this. I'll be right in," he said, setting the bags down and walking away.

I pulled our luggage in one suitcase at a time and left them in the entry before following my ears to the music playing from the back patio. I hadn't seen Fred and Margaret in two years, but we'd kept in touch through Christmas and birthday cards. They'd never met a date of mine, and I wanted to give them a heads-up before I introduced Jeff.

On the way here, I'd told him about them, but he didn't seem to pay much attention. His work had been blowing his phone up all day, and I understood that more than anyone. Business always came first.

I brushed my hand down the back of the leather couch in the living room as I walked toward the back. Blankets were strewn about the floor, pillows weren't fluffed, and the room smelled like stale pizza and beer.

I wrinkled my nose and stepped over a pile of wet towels, heaped in a puddle at the back door. Outside, the wind picked up, lapping the waves against the rocky shoreline. At the end of the dock sat three figures with their feet splashing in the water. One of them, a woman, threw her head back and laughed.

I squinted but couldn't make out what kind of bandits were living in my lake house.

"Fred? Margaret?" I shouted above the music, making my way down the cliffside.

They turned toward me.

"Madison!" Jeff called, jogging to catch up. "Sorry. These idiots can't figure out how to do anything when I'm out of the office."

I paused mid-step, staring at Seth, a woman I'd not met before, and that douche-bag Preston in disbelief.

"Madison?" Jeff followed my gaze, landing on Preston. He puffed out his chest, nearly popping a stitch on his tailored button-up. "What the fuck is he doing here?"

"I don't know." I blew out a breath.

Seth switched off the speaker. "Madison?"

All three rose to their feet and began to walk up the dock.

Jeff put his arm around me and held me close in an almost-painful iron grip.

"I didn't know you were coming into town. You should have told me!" Seth said before he reached us.

"How was I to know you'd be here? You're usually … busy." I eyed the woman.

She wore a basic black wrap around her tiny waist, accentuating her thick hips. Her breasts spilled over a matching bikini top. Preston side-eyed her cleavage but composed himself once my brother introduced her.

"I brought my girlfriend over for a quick getaway. It looks like you're doing the same. Melanie, this is my sister, Madison. And her …"

"Date. His name is Jeff. A pleasure to meet you, Melanie." I extended my hand while Jeff and my brother exchanged formalities.

"You too! I've heard all about you. Not from this one." She nudged Seth with her elbow. "But this one." She rolled her eyes, landing on Preston.

Preston's face turned a crimson shade of red. He glared at me, then Jeff, and back to me again. I felt the hate simmering under his gaze.

"Oh! And this is my best bro, Preston." Seth clapped Preston on the shoulder.

"We've met." Jeff's tone came out sickeningly sweet and edged with steel.

My feet buckled as I realized Jeff's jealousy meant he'd already caught the feels.

Preston drew himself up to his full height and smiled, setting my teeth on edge.

"Yep. I know Jeff. We used to tag-team projects back in the day," Preston said.

Jeff drew in a sharp breath and rolled his shoulders.

"Anyway, it's nice to meet you, Melanie. We have to unpack. Let's catch up later. We'll take the upstairs guest room." I tugged on Jeff's sleeve, rushing us far away from them as fast as I could.

"Uh, that's where Preston's staying." Seth put up a hand, stopping me.

"Not anymore." I lifted my chin and waited, challenging him.

Melanie smacked Preston's arm with the back of her hand.

"Give them that room! You don't need that big ol' bed by yourself! Besides, don't you want to be downstairs with your bro and his new girl? You can take one of those bunk beds, and maybe you and Seth can have a slumber party, staying up all night, talking shit about me." Melanie laughed until a faint blush crept across her freckled cheeks.

"Whatever. I'm not staying much longer. I'll move my stuff. I'm used to being in different beds anyway. No telling whose bed I'll end up in." Preston shrugged before jogging away.

"Poor kid wasn't able to snag a summer fling for this escape." Melanie jerked her head back toward the water. "He's probably really going to feel like a third wheel now."

"He'll be fine!" Seth assured her. "He'll have a woman back here in no time. Just wait. You'll see. He's infamous for picking up chicks. Isn't he, Madison? She knows. She grew up with him too. He's indestructible. Don't let his pout fool you."

The heat coming off Jeff's body was stifling.

"I don't pity him," I said, leaving.

"Will you be around for dinner? We were thinking about roasting hot dogs and marshmallows at the firepit if you two want to join!" Melanie called out to our backs.

"We'll see!" I answered, not stopping to think about it.

We made it back up the hill and to the patio before Jeff grabbed my arm and stopped me.

"You grew up with him? So, what? You two are close?" he asked through gritted teeth.

I yanked my arm from his grip. "I told you we knew each other! I didn't know I had to go into details. Why are you upset with me? If I had known he'd be here, I wouldn't have come. This is supposed to be my time to relax! Not deal with that asshole. Or any asshole." I drew my brows together and stuck out my jaw.

Jeff reached out, resting his palms on my shoulders. "I'm not upset with you." His tone grew soft, but the fury that blazed in his eyes remained unchanged. "It was a shock, is all—the man who … who … look, I saw your face when he was behind you. I was staring at you. And you were staring back at him. Not me, and I was the one in front of you. I got a little jealous. Thought maybe there was something more there between you two. I didn't ask because I figured that was a one-time thing and we'd moved on. I didn't know you two were close."

"It was a one-time thing. And that's disgusting for you to even suggest I'd care for that nimrod. I can't stand him!"

"Then, why'd you let him fuck you in the ass?"

I clenched my fists at my sides, fighting off the urge to punch him in his face. I didn't know what douche-baginess had overtaken him, but I wasn't going to tolerate it.

"I moved my stuff. The room's all yours, Madison." Preston emerged from the back of the house and came toward us. His eyes traveled up from my balled fists to Jeff's sneer. He shifted his weight on his feet. "Everything okay?"

"She's fine," Jeff snapped, cutting his eyes to mine.

"I didn't ask if she was fine. I asked if everything was okay. And she doesn't look fine. She looks like she's about to punch someone. And if I know Madison, that someone is you—or me. Probably both. She's taken us on at the same time before though, so she should be used to it."

"Preston! It's really not the time." I stopped him.

Jeff stepped into Preston, nearly knocking him back.

"We don't joke about it anymore. We don't talk about it anymore. We don't think about it anymore. That night is done and over with. She's mine, and we're together now. Got it?" Jeff asked.

Preston stepped back and twisted his mouth into an evil grin. "I wouldn't touch your girlfriend with a ten-foot dick. But if you ever threaten me like that again, I'll fucking knock out those alarmingly bright teeth of yours and let you gum on my cock next time. You can ask your girlfriend how I like it."

"Fuck," I growled, moving in between them. "Both of you, knock it off. We're adults. The past stays in the past. I'm forgetting it ever happened, and so are both of you if you know what's best for you. Jeff, I will send your ass off so quick. And, you"—I cut my eyes to Preston—"I will cut you in your fucking sleep. Do not test me. Get over yourselves. Besides, I've had better a better fuck with a middle-aged man in a clown costume than with you two meatwads."

I stomped away, leaving them both in my dust.

"Wait!" Jeff followed me.

But I didn't stop until I reached the bedroom, where I flung the door shut after him, rattling the pictures on the wood-paneled walls. The room still smelled of Preston's cologne—cedar, musk, and money. In his rush to clear the area, he hadn't bothered to make the bed.

"How dare you! We haven't had the girlfriend discussion. And at the rate you're going, to hell I'm yours!" I crossed my arms across my chest and stuck out my hip.

"I overstepped. I panicked and overstepped!" Jeff threw his hands in the air as he walked toward the bed and plopped down. "Baby, I promise you, I won't do that again. I just wanted him to know there wasn't going to be any more shenanigans between you two. I'm so sorry. So, so sorry. Do you forgive me?"

I studied the guilt in his eyes before responding.

"And?" I asked.

"And?" He swallowed hard. "And you aren't my girlfriend—yet. But I promise to prove I'm worthy of you when that time comes. Sorry I mislabeled you."

"I make my own labels."

"I know." He opened his mouth but quickly shut it again.

"Don't ever forget it."

"I won't. This is your vacation, Madison. I won't let some jackass ruin it. Me or him. Now, come over here, and let's start over." His tongue slid across his lips, wetting them while he began to unbutton his pants.

"Good. It's my vacation. So, spoil me." I shuffled my feet toward him as he rose and grabbed my hips, throwing me on the bed in one quick movement.

He tore out of his jacket and button-up while I flung my clothes off and onto the floor—not caring that my designer silk blouse wouldn't recover from the dirt on these antique floorboards. My mind wasn't on fashion or drama. I only needed one thing, and he was standing right in front of me with an expression of raw, filthy, rough lust—just how I liked it. I didn't know what exactly I was being punished for, but I spread my legs and gladly welcomed whatever I had coming to me.

PRESTON

I cracked open a bottle of beer and propped my feet on the side of the firepit. Melanie sat on the bench, curled under a blanket with Seth—no doubt rubbing his johnson underneath. They hadn't kept their hands off each other since I arrived. It was gross. I'd never seen googly eyes on my bro before, and I didn't like it. Melanie practically had him in the palm of her hand.

"So, Preston Lancaster, the playboy of the South, couldn't find a summer fling. I find that hard to believe." Seth took a swig of beer before offering it to his girlfriend.

She threw back the covers and took it, gulping the entire bottle and licking her lips. "Probably because he's been through 'em all."

I drew in a sharp breath. I hadn't even been here for two days, and already, his girl knew me better than anyone. She roasted me like I roasted my frat brothers, Madison, and anyone else who crossed my path.

Seth bit his knuckles and stifled a laugh.

"I'll have you know … you're probably right." I shrugged, guzzling the beer down the way I had during my impressive keg-stand days back home. "It was either that or word got out that I'm not looking for a wife. Every chick wants to bed and wed these days. It's not for me."

"What's wrong with being in a committed relationship?" Melanie asked.

Seth's eyes grew wide beside her as he subtly shook his head in my direction.

I pulled a marshmallow out of the bag beside me and shoved it on the metal stick.

"One woman for the rest of my life? No, thanks. That'd get old quick." I shoved the marshmallow into the fire, crisping the edges until it began to smoke.

"Not if you met the right woman," she said.

"Yeah, it would. It always gets old, even with the right woman. That's when you have to work hard at it and do the *spice up your life* bullshit. I'd rather it be natural, and that shit fades." I pulled the flaming marshmallow from the fire and blew it out in one puff.

Seth sat in silence, busying himself with a loose string on the blanket.

"It doesn't fade. It just changes into a much, much deeper feeling. It's not as exciting, but it's more fulfilling. Nothing wrong with that." She covered herself back up and curled her feet across Seth's lap.

"I beg to differ, miss. I'll take new booty over—" I said.

A loud scream pierced through our conversation, interrupting my bro-code explanation.

"Ah. She finally took a shower." I smirked, forgetting where I was at in the conversation.

"Dude. What did you do?" Seth sighed, rubbing his palms across his face.

"Preston! You asshole!" Madison screamed, running toward us and stopping inches from me. Her skin glowed a sickly bright orange color, even in the dim firelight.

Melanie gasped.

I threw back my head and laughed.

"How the fuck am I supposed to go anywhere like this? You fucker! You're going to pay for this, you know!" Madison grabbed the bag of marshmallows and dumped them over my head before picking up a handful and hurling them at my face.

"Gah! Stop! That's just payback. For everything! Relax. It'll scrub off in, like, a week. I think. Melanie should know." I blocked my face from a pummel of marshmallows.

"Is that my self-tanner?" Melanie cut her eyes to mine.

"He put it in the soap bottle!" Madison cried. "I was showering, and when I came out, I was … was … this!" She swept her hands over her body, wrapped in a dress that looked like a giant pillowcase made from the fabric of my grandma's couch.

Seth and I burst into laughter. I doubled over in my chair, grabbing my sides, trying to catch my breath.

Melanie shook her head. "You owe me a bottle, Preston. That stuff's expensive!" She turned toward Madison. "Looks like he just started a prank war. Time to put on our thinking caps. Here, might as well." She reached in the cooler and pulled out a beer, popping the top and passing it to Madison.

"Oh, my thinking cap's on! It's been on. You're lucky I didn't get it in my hair, asshole. Otherwise, I'd throw you into that fire!" She plopped herself down in the Adirondack chair across from me, crossing her legs at the ankles.

"Did Jeff use it too?" I bit back the hope that crept into my voice.

"No. You'd be dead by now if he did."

I blew a breath out of my nose.

"Where is he? You two have to tell me how you met! We were discussing the merits of having a steady relationship," Melanie said.

"I'm sure he'll be down soon. He had a work call. We had to cut dinner short. But now, I guess I'll be eating at home for the next week." Madison narrowed her eyes at me and took a long gulp of beer.

"It's not that bad. What shade is that, babe?" Seth turned toward Melanie. "À la traffic cone?"

She smacked him with the back of her hand.

"Here, have another beer, Preston, and tell us all about your bachelor lifestyle you can't resist." Melanie handed me a bottle and winked at Madison.

"This should be interesting," Madison said, settling into her seat and blending in with the fire in between us.

"I'm a bro for life. What else is there to say? I like babes. They like me. I'll keep it up until I'm a silver fox. Then, I'll keep it up some more," I said.

"I can see it now. You're going to start balding at twenty-eight, get a beer gut at thirty, knock someone up at thirty-four, and have three more kids by the time you're forty. You'll be married with a dad bod, working the same nine-to-five as other hopeless dickwads. Your 401(k) will get more action than you, except your wife will divorce you and take it all before you come close to retiring. Then, you'll die a lonely, old fart." Madison scuffed her foot across the dirt and smiled.

"Oh. Okay. Wow. That was a nasty burn." Melanie fanned herself.

"I call it as I see it." Madison held her beer up in mock salute, focusing over my shoulder.

I heard his obnoxiously loud footsteps before I saw him. The way his feet stomped across the yard could wake the dead. It was as if he wanted to be heard, seen, and worshipped. I rolled my eyes and took another drink.

"What do we have here? We tellin' ghost stories?" Jeff asked, walking over to Madison and sitting beside her. He pulled a bottle of whiskey from a bag before reaching across and planting a kiss on her forehead.

Forehead? That's a love thing. No one does that unless they're serious! She can't be that serious.

"No ghost stories. Ghosted stories maybe. But nothing too scary. We're a boring bunch." Seth yawned, putting his arm around Melanie's shoulders.

"Lucky for you all then, I brought the party—Willow Oak Reserve. Only fourteen cases of these were produced this year. I'd pour us a glass, but what's the fun in that? Just sip and pass." Jeff twisted the top off of the bottle, took a swig, and passed it to me.

I drank it in one swallow of smooth liquid fire.

"Gah," I said, handing it to Melanie.

She waved it away and passed it to Seth.

"It's good." My voice came out an octave too high, my vocal cords scorched.

Jeff smirked.

Seth tossed back a sip and let out a howl before passing it to Madison. Jeff intercepted the bottle and held it from her reach.

"What?" Madison asked, leaving her hand hanging in the air in a *give me* gesture.

"You think you should?" Jeff tilted his head before nodding at her beer.

Madison's face flushed even brighter. She folded her arms and sat back in her chair.

An awkward silence fell upon us like a heavy, wet blanket—stifling and uncomfortable as fuck.

"So, Jeff, I was asking Madison how you two met. Care to share?" Melanie caught Jeff's attention.

He peered over the bottle and took a drink before answering, "We met at the gym. She followed me into a spin class once and fell flat on her face. Remember that?" He looked at Madison and laughed.

"Ha-ha," she answered.

"Anyway, after that, I asked her out. I figured any woman willing to fall off a bike and get right back on was determined. And I like that—determination. It's sexy. And, well, look at her. She's gorgeous. She makes me look good." He passed the bottle to me, avoiding my gaze.

I swatted away a mosquito buzzing in my ear and took two big gulps, burning my tongue.

I can't believe she brought an asshat like Jeff to the lake house. At least when I make fun of her, I …

I peered at Madison and lost my train of thought before giving the whiskey to Seth.

"The gym. Sounds like the perfect meet-cute. I met this one at the doctor's office where I work." Melanie stuck her pointy chin out in Seth's direction. "He came in for a flu shot. I don't know any men who do that without their wives begging them to. But I checked his paperwork, and he was single. So, I asked him out, breaking all protocol. I at least waited until after I stuck him though."

"You didn't get the flu bug, but it looks like you got the love bug instead. Cheers to that!" Jeff smiled a stupidly perfect smile.

I rubbed my face, unsure if I'd heard him right. Seth hadn't mentioned anything about love.

Gross.

"What was that?" Seth asked me.

"Did I say something out loud?" I cringed, rubbing my sweaty palms down my shorts.

"You mumbled." Melanie reached over and patted my knee. "I'm a nurse, by the way. Just so you know," both of her heads told me.

"It's the whiskey. It's nearly double proof of most whiskeys. It sneaks up on you really quick." Jeff passed the bottle back to me and tilted his head, challenging me.

I didn't lose at anything—even if it put me into a coma.

"I got an idea! Let's play a drinking game—Never Have I Ever." Madison perked up, shooting me a mischievous smile from across the fire.

"Let's do it," Melanie said, opening another beer and clinking it against Seth's bottle.

"Hit me." I glared at Madison.

"Never have I ever lost a bet." Madison grinned.

Seth and Melanie each took a drink of their beer. I reached for the whiskey and tossed it back.

Jeff tapped his annoyingly chiseled jawline. "Never have I ever been arrested."

Seth and I looked at each other, exchanged laughs, and took another drink.

"What on earth? You never told me that!" Melanie said. "I bet it was together too."

"Yep," I answered. "Never have I ever cheated on a partner."

"Oh, you're so full of shit!" Madison rolled her eyes in my direction.

"It's true!" I held up my hands and swayed in my seat, catching myself before diving headfirst into the fire.

"I don't believe that for a second," she huffed.

An owl hooted from somewhere beside us. Or I was hearing things. At this point, it could go either way. The alcohol fogged my brain under its fuzzy spell.

Jeff picked up the bottle of whiskey and drank.

"Really?" Madison scoffed, wrinkling her nose at her douche-bag boyfriend.

"A really, really long time ago. It's a long story. At least I'm honest. Anyway, next!" Jeff said, clearing his throat.

I caught Madison's eye above the flames and grinned. She flipped me the finger.

"Never have I ever gotten dirty in public." Melanie sighed.

Everyone, except her, took a drink.

"You were adventurous then, and now what? You're holding out on me." She narrowed her eyes at Seth.

"Nope. I'm still pretty adventurous and surprising. Check it. Never have I ever eaten the groceries and didn't like it." Seth danced in his seat and wiggled his brows at Melanie.

"Fuck." I laughed, taking another drink of whiskey. The alcohol didn't even burn anymore.

"Oh, gross. I don't want to know what my brother does in bed. Thanks!" Madison gagged.

Jeff took the bottle back from me and put it to his lips.

"What's groceries?" Melanie asked.

"Ass. He said he likes to eat ass," I slurred.

"Oh. Well, bottoms up then." She shrugged, toasting Seth and taking a sip of her beer.

We erupted in laughter.

"I'm a nurse. I know when germs aren't safe! Besides—" Melanie started.

"Stop!" Madison pleaded, gasping for breath between laughs. Tears streamed down her face. "I can't. Just don't … ugh! Never have I ever gone skinny-dipping!"

Everyone took a drink, except Madison. Of course, little Miss Goody–Two Shoes wouldn't be caught dead naked in public. But she had a wild side, and I was going to expose it. I had to keep her on her toes.

"Never have I ever experimented with the same sex," Jeff said.

Melanie took a sip of her beer.

"You've been holdin' out on me!" Seth blurted.

"We should communicate more," she said.

I tried to picture Melanie making out with another woman, but my brain turned to mush.

"Never have I ever given someone a dirty sanchez." I hiccuped.

"Ew! What the fuck?" Seth cried, pushing himself back in his seat.

Madison peered at me over the flames and took a sip of beer.

Seth gave a girlish scream, and I almost fell out of my chair.

"Are you serious?" Jeff asked Madison.

"It's not what you're thinking." She waved him away and flipped me the bird again.

"Never have I ever had a threesome." Melanie's body split into two and came back together again before I could bring the whiskey to my lips and drink.

Madison and Jeff hesitated before reaching for the bottle and drinking. Jeff's six eyes drifted to mine. I looked away and smirked. At least, I thought I'd smirked. I couldn't feel my face anymore.

"No way. Jealous! I've always wanted a gang bang myself, but—" Melanie said.

"What?" Seth sat up in his seat. "You do?"

"Every woman does," Madison answered, toasting Melanie above the fire.

"Never have I ever considered sharing the woman I love." Seth pouted.

"What? Did you just say that four-letter word we haven't exchanged yet?" Melanie's mouth dropped open.

"Yep. I love you. And I'm not sharing. Deal with it," Seth said.

Melanie squealed and crawled onto his lap.

"I think I'm going to be sick," I said, leaning my elbows on my knees and cradling my head to stop the world from spinning.

"Never have I ever ruined someone else's vacation." Madison squinted in my direction, drawing her sharp-pointed fingernail across her throat.

She'd already known the answer to every question she asked, and this well-played game was just another challenge. If I wasn't so proud, I would have told her that her method of payback was borderline genius.

I pushed myself back up, leaning forward, and tried to swipe the bottle next to me. But I missed, fell to the ground, and passed out.

Madison had gone too far in the prank war. She'd finally tried to kill me.

The smell of breakfast roused me from an epic, hellish hangover. I winced with each loud pop of bacon grease, sounding off like a cannonball inside my aching head.

"Mom?" I groaned, rubbing my eyes before opening them.

The sunlight streamed through the massive living room windows in a blinding bright light.

"Mommy isn't here to save you this time," Madison said in a singsong voice.

"Why am I here?" I asked, struggling for my eyes to adjust to the room. A pile of pillows surrounded me like a fort.

"You couldn't exactly make it to your room, you big doofus." Madison stepped into my view, crunching a piece of bacon between her teeth. Her skin was the color of a biohazardous orange.

"Why? What happened?" I croaked and swallowed hard, wincing at my raw throat.

"Ahem." Margaret, the Sheffields' housekeeper, walked over, handing me a glass of water.

She shook her head in the devastating disappointment that only a mother could give. I'd known Margaret and her family since I was little. She'd become much more like a second mom to me than even Ms. Sheffield herself. Now and then, she'd help me with a problem I had over my summer stays, and when my mom had been diagnosed with cancer, she'd checked in regularly, knitting my mom this or baking her that.

I took the water from Margaret and guzzled it down.

"Good morning." I squinted, handing her back the glass with a shaky hand.

"I wish I could say I was surprised to find you here in this state, Preston, but I'm not. You're going to grow up one day; I just know it. But that isn't today or anytime soon by the looks of you." Her silvering hair fell limp around her face. She rubbed her wrinkled neck and turned to leave.

"By the looks of me? That bad, huh?" I asked Madison.

"See for yourself," she said, snatching the blanket off of me.

I looked down at my legs. The left lay wrapped entirely in a cast.

"What?!" I yelled, wiggling to try to get off the couch. But the weight of the cast and the pillow fort made it hard for me to budge.

"Don't move! The doctor said it's still fragile! You might have to wear it for another eighteen months!" Madison gently patted it before grabbing a remote and turning on the television.

"Eighteen months! For fuck's sake! What did I do last night?" I cried, staring at the signatures on my cast.

Seth had drawn a penis, Madison had written *XOXO*, and Jeff ... he had drawn a smile.

"You don't remember?" she asked, flipping through the channels.

"I remember you trying to kill me! So, this"—I pointed at my cast—"is your fault!" I pressed my fingertips to my temples, steadying myself before I got sick. The taste of bile lingered on my tongue.

"I think not. I didn't shove alcohol down your throat!" She crossed her arms and sat at my feet, plopping herself down hard toward the end of the couch and making us both bounce.

"Don't be so rough! You said I'm fragile! Agh!" A wave of panic washed over me.

My dick.

I reached down, slipping my hand under my boxers and making sure my dick was okay. I squished it in my palm, satisfied that at least it was still attached even if it felt a little sad.

"Relax. It's still there." She rolled her eyes and turned the television off before tossing the remote back on the table.

"What's all this commotion? Is that bacon I smell? I bet Margaret's cooking again! Yes!" Melanie fist-pumped the air. Her makeup was messily smeared all over her face.

If she looked that bad, I must've looked like death.

"Melanie! You're a nurse. How did I do this? What did the doctor say? Can I move? Will it hurt?" I wiped a bead of sweat from my brow.

"Oh! You're up! Good. Well, let's start with what you can't do. You can't walk, work out, go to the potty on your own, or have sex." Melanie put her hands on her hips and shot me a look of disappointment. She'd make a great mom one day.

"I'm going to be sick." I put my hands to my face and moaned.

"I think you got everything out last night. On my shoes." Melanie narrowed her eyes.

"Ah, well, I think there are some things you can do to help yourself feel better faster and heal your leg," Madison chimed in, rising from the couch.

"I can get this off faster?" I asked.

"Yes." Madison twirled her hair around her finger.

"How?"

"You quit fucking with me." Her lips parted in a sinister smile.

I looked at Melanie and scratched my head.

"I'm getting breakfast. This is between you two. I did my part. Besides, it's payback for my best pair of shoes and my expensive-as-hell tanning lotion." Melanie crossed her heart and ran out of the room toward the kitchen.

"I'm so damn confused. Can you just tell me exactly how I fucked up last night and how I can get this cast off my leg as quickly as possible? Then, maybe get Seth to help me to the bathroom, please."

I looked away. I didn't have the energy to argue with Madison. She was the type who brought a gun to a knife fight, and I showed up this morning without a weapon, save for my big-ass fucking plastered cast.

"Sure. You just passed out last night after not being able to handle your whiskey. Seth and Jeff carried you in and put you to bed here. But I asked for Melanie's help to pay your ass back for this bullshit tan. So, she had some supplies in her car, and we taped your leg up to look like you had broken it. You're fine. You can go to the bathroom yourself if you can walk in that thing. I win. The end."

She let out a dramatic yawn and skipped away before I could tell her how much I hated her.

I mustered up every draining ounce of energy I had and pulled myself up. I tapped my cast to make sure she wasn't pulling my leg again, ironically, but I felt nothing. I barely remembered a thing from last night, and I didn't trust Madison with the truth. I slammed my hand down on the cast and still felt nothing.

Seth appeared from the hall, shuffling his feet across the stone floor. He looked like he'd crawled out of a grave.

"Ugh. I tried to get up early to help you out of this thing before they woke up. Sorry, man. They insisted. I can't tell my girlfriend no. She said you deserved it after what you did to Madison. Have you seen her? She looks awful! Like a fucking glass of gnarly orange juice." He grabbed ahold of my arm and hoisted me up.

"What about bros before hos, man? What the fuck?" I swayed, fumbling to catch my footing with a straight and heavy leg.

"I'm in love. It makes me do stupid shit!"

"Well, you never needed an excuse to do stupid shit before!" I huffed, jerking my arm away from him. "And you wouldn't have let some chick do something like this to me either. So much for our bromance."

"Now, that's not fair. We were all wasted last night! I tried to get down here early and fix it, but—"

"Yeah, yeah." I waved him away and hobbled toward the kitchen in search of something sharp to cut this iron shackle off of me. But as I rounded the corner, a wave of nausea hit me. I lost my balance and fell to the floor in a loud crash, right at Madison's neon feet.

"Damn it, Madison! This isn't over!" I yelled, catching a quick glance under her robe as she stepped over me.

She wasn't wearing panties. Her smooth, silken pussy flashed me like a smile. My dick sparked alive. For a moment, I forgot I was pissed until she opened her mouth again.

"Aw. Now, you aren't mad, are ya?" she called over her shoulder, leaving me lying on the floor in a confusion of horny anger.

I gritted my teeth and pulled myself back up. If Madison thought she'd won, she was mistaken. The games were just getting started.

MADISON

I tied my running sneakers and set off before dawn to clear my head. Before college, I'd wake early most mornings at the lake house and jog down the road to our local coffee shop, The Daily Grind, on the pier. The old Italian couple who owned it, Gloria and Louis, knew me by name, and most mornings, my iced Americano was ready and waiting. But I hadn't seen them in years, and I wasn't really in the mood to visit with anyone either.

For the first time in our relationship, Jeff had gone to bed later than me. Usually, we headed to bed together, fucked, and fell asleep, spooning. But yesterday, he'd shot me down to stay up late, working. I wasn't upset about his job. I'd have done the same thing if I wasn't technically on vacation. But the goofy grin slathered over his face when he was texting on his phone had seemed suspicious. It was the same goofy grin I'd caught myself wearing when he texted me.

I stepped out of the front door and planted one foot on the ground in front of me, dipping my hips down into a deep stretch. The air hung heavy with the smell of wet earth and fresh mulch. Our landscaper had recently overhauled our massive gardens with a modern twist, as per my mother's request. Even though Liza was always too busy to vacation at the lake house these days, she still had to keep up appearances and trends for her ego.

I turned away from the lake house and hit the pavement. I hadn't run outside since I'd been here last, years ago. My morning jogs used to be spent in the university gym on an archaic treadmill, squeezed in between rows of squeaking elliptical machines. And these days, I skipped running altogether for spin. But I missed the time in my childhood when I'd wake up early to train for a track meet or to work off Margaret's famous cinnamon rolls. Life had been much simpler back then than it was this morning.

I bit my tongue and glared up at the purpling sky, pushing back the sorrow that'd hit me straight in the chest when Margaret confessed her cancer diagnosis. One minute, we were laughing at my epic prank on Preston, and the next, she was bracing herself against the sink, a sickening cough racking her lungs. I thought Margaret was only choking on her laughter or had seasonal allergies until I saw the look of dread cross Melanie's face. I knew then that my new nurse friend thought this was something more serious. And it hadn't taken much convincing for Margaret to tell us the problem.

I pushed my heels into the ground and sprinted, winding down the driveway and toward the street. The road leading to our neighborhood veered off in a path that ran parallel to the lake and into the small fishing town of Cloverly.

When my dad had purchased our lake lot, we'd come out every weekend, checking on the new build. Liza custom-designed our home as one of her first commissioned projects—paid for by her then-husband, my dad.

But shortly after, he was caught with his assistant, and hell hath no fury like a woman scorned. My mother took her rage—and his investments—and ran with them. She'd turned her feelings off and her business plans on, and that was how the Sheffield dynasty was born.

After our first summer at the lake, Margaret and Fred had come into the picture when my mother realized she couldn't do it all herself anymore.

I breathed hard through my nose, pushing myself as fast as I could away from the house and down toward the fishing pier. The Daily Grind opened early to serve breakfast to the hungry fishermen who visited the lake for competitions during the summer months. My guilty pleasure was sitting at a corner table, watching them and listening to their small talk.

They spoke of their wives, their families, and especially their recent catches. I didn't know a damn thing about fishing, but their simple takes on life were refreshing. It wouldn't take too long before I grew bored and headed back home to my not-so-simple life and sank into the comfort of familiar luxury. I liked to read or learn about other walks of life but not live them. My heart remained true to my elite roots.

I'd spotted Fred once, grabbing two coffees to go, the summer I was fifteen. His face grew animated as he explained his wife's battle with their problematic squirrels. His voice carried with a soft bounce each time he said her name, as if just whispering her into the air lifted his mood. I tried to do the same with my crush when I went back home, but I didn't feel the same joy that had played across Fred's face. Instead, I'd felt nothing, and I'd felt nothing for men ever since—until now.

Jeff was everything I'd wanted in a man, and I was falling fast. But something was off, and I couldn't put my finger on it. He made me feel amazing one moment and like I was the worst person on the planet the next—not intentionally, of course. At least, I didn't think so. His standards were much higher than any other man's I'd dated, and for once in my dating life, I had to work at a relationship. I wanted him to look at me the way Fred looked at Margaret. But instead, I couldn't read Jeff's expressions, and sometimes, I thought they looked like Preston's—full of hate and annoyance.

I kept running, picking up speed downhill until I heard the water lapping against the pier. The sun barely peeked over the horizon, and already, men were untying their boats and speeding off across the other's wake, each competing for the prized fishing spots. I knew because it was the same every year and one of the most significant events in Cloverly.

Seth and Preston had entered the competition once during our last summer at the lake house. But instead of hopping in the boat to fish, they rented a yacht to entice a few low-end social media models to pose on it for free. In return, they'd gotten to hang with bikini babes. I still didn't see what was in it for the models.

I slowed my run to a brisk walk as I edged closer to the coffee shop.

"Madison!" Jeff called from behind me.

I turned to catch him running toward me before nearly collapsing. He rested his palms on his knees, bending his tall frame forward and catching his breath.

"Hey! I thought you were asleep. I didn't want to wake you." I reached out, rubbing his back.

"Anyone ever tell you that you're like a damn cheetah? I couldn't even keep up!"

"A tigress, not a cheetah. But I'll take either. Sorry. I just needed to … run. Clears my head like spin, except this"—I motioned toward the lake and pier—"brings it to another level. Nostalgia, I guess."

"Why're you up so early anyway? I thought only I got up this early to exercise."

"I always get up this early to exercise when I'm here and sometimes at home. I changed my workout schedule to include spin—and you," I said as I unzipped my running jacket and revealed my Minx brand moisture-wicking athletic top.

"Oh. I thought maybe you were trying to get away from me." He reached out, trailing his knuckles over my cheek.

"Why would I do that?" I asked, pulling away.

His phone buzzed in his pocket.

"Ugh! One sec." He held up a finger and answered, walking down the pier and out of earshot.

I stared off into the distance, watching the sunrise and noticing the coloring of the horizon matched my fake-tanned skin.

"Okay. Clients." Jeff shrugged, jogging back to me.

"I understand. Come on. I need caffeine." I jerked my head toward the door and swung it open.

The smell of maple syrup and freshly brewed coffee knocked me in the face, wrapping around my senses like a warm blanket.

"I missed this place," I sighed, stepping into a crowd of old men bogged down with wading boots, ball caps, fishing vests, and anxious rivalry.

"Come here often?" Jeff asked, peering over everyone's heads.

"All the time, back in the day." My eyes darted to my favorite corner table. "Hey! I'm going to grab that table. Can you get me an iced Americano, please? And ugh, I'll indulge. Guess I'll take one of their pastries. You choose which. They're all delicious!"

"Are you sure you want that much sugar in the morning? You just worked out. Kind of defeats the purpose." He rolled his eyes.

"I ... yeah, I'm hungry," I said, wrinkling my nose.

He raised his eyebrows and left, pushing his way to the back of the line and leaving me standing in a state of confusion. I'd never had issues with eating before. I ate when I was hungry, and I didn't when I wasn't. I never ate my feelings or out of boredom, and I worked damn hard for my physique. Maybe I couldn't measure up to Jeff's Roman god stature, but I thought I did well for myself in the fitness department. Hell, I was even designing an entire line of fitness gear.

I rubbed the back of my neck and made my way toward the corner table. Crumbs were scattered across the tabletop, and a dollop of ketchup was smeared across the seat.

"I'll get it, dear. Don't sit down just yet!" Gloria walked toward me and began wiping down the furniture with a wet dishrag.

"Gloria." I smiled, greeting my old friend.

She threw the dishrag over her shoulder and adjusted her glasses, peering into my face. Her silver hair was swept back in the usual granny bun that she'd worn since I first met her nearly a decade ago.

"Oh my word! It's Madison Sheffield. Honey! Honey! Come quick!" she shouted above the crowd of grumbling men.

Jeff caught my eye and tilted his head, watching our interaction.

Louis rushed over to us.

"What's wrong? Something on fire? What is it, woman?" He threw his hands in the air.

"She's back!" Gloria pointed her chin in my direction. Her eyes crinkled, peeking from over the top of her black frames.

"Mamma mia! It's Madison!" Louis threw his arms around my shoulders and smushed me into his doughy chest. "You've come back!" He pushed me away, holding me at arm's length for inspection.

"And goodness! You need some meat on those bones. You're too skinny! Too skinny! What are they feeding you at school? Ice chips? Sit. Let me bring you pie." Gloria pulled the chair from under the table and ushered me into it.

I looked back at Jeff and smirked, but his attention remained on the younger girl taking his order. He was leaning into the counter, flashing her a boyish grin. The same one he'd flashed me when we first met.

"I'm okay. My ... boyfriend is getting me something." I cringed at the word I'd dared to speak aloud.

"Boyfriend?" Louis swiveled on his heels, took a quick peek at the only man my age in the coffee shop, and turned back to me. "He's a giant! He's been eating all your food!"

"No, no. I eat! I just get busy and forget sometimes, is all. But I do eat!" I laughed, waving away his concern. "Look, here comes food now!"

Jeff made his way toward us with a plate of dry toast and two iced coffees.

"Uh, thanks," I said as he set the plate in front of me. "Jeff, this is Gloria and Louis. They own the place. And this is Jeff." I pressed my lips together and picked at a piece of crust.

"Pleasure to meet you. Lovely place you have here!" He wiped his hands down his pants and shook their hands before settling into his seat.

Louis eyed him skeptically.

"Jeff, your girlfriend is like a daughter to us. Tell her she isn't looking healthy! She's skinny, and she needs more than toast! How will she ever bear children with no hips?" Gloria said, shifting on her loafers.

I sucked in a breath through my teeth and tried to cool my reddening cheeks.

"Ah." Jeff chuckled before taking a long sip of coffee. "She's beautiful though, isn't she?"

I lifted my gaze to meet Gloria, who wore a puzzled look buried in the folds of her face. My stomach twisted into a knot.

"Of course she is. Such a lucky man." Louis rubbed the gray scruff across his jowl.

"I need backup!" shouted the young lady at the counter. The line had grown out the door.

"We'll catch up later," Gloria said, tugging Louis away from our table.

Jeff kept guzzling his coffee, not-so-subtly looking back toward the order counter.

"Nice couple," he said.

"Do you have a problem?" I asked, drumming my fingernails across the tabletop.

"Huh?"

"With me. That little comment about not wanting me to get fat."

"What? I never said that!"

"You did. And I asked for a pastry, not this." I pushed the plate of toast away.

"I was trying to help. You were working out, and I thought I was being helpful! Wow. Don't be so dramatic. You're overreacting!" His voice rose to a high pitch, drawing a nearby customer's attention.

"Maybe. I've just had a rough morning. I'll probably go home and crawl back into bed." I looked toward the Exit sign.

"Whatever you need to do to be less crabby, do it." He made a long slurping noise through his straw.

I grabbed my coffee, stood up from my chair, and began to walk away.

"I'll see you two later!" I shouted at Gloria and Louis before disappearing out the door and back into the fresh air.

A heavy fog had seemingly come out of nowhere, blanketing the town in a misty haze.

"Wait! I'm sorry," Jeff yelled, catching up to me. "I guess I'm crabby too in the morning. I didn't mean to come off like that."

"Maybe you should get more sleep instead of staying shackled to your phone all damn night, grinning at whoever the fuck you're texting."

"Excuse me? Don't you trust me? I was talking to my team. My fucking team, Madison."

"Oh yeah? Show me." I jutted my chin out, challenging him.

"Yeah, right. We aren't at that level." He dismissed me and continued walking up the path toward the street.

"You called me your girlfriend, and you can't show me your phone? Ha. Guilty." I blew a breath out of my nose.

"I wasn't even talking to anyone last night! I have no idea what you're going on about. You're just trying to pick a fight."

"Yes, you were! I saw you grinning at your phone like you were talking to a naked, hot chick!"

"A naked, hot chick? You're nuts!"

"No. I saw it."

"You need your eyes checked. You saw nothing."

"So, I'm lying?"

"Or you're batshit crazy."

I swallowed back tears, trying to think if maybe I had been tired last night and mistaken what I saw. Or perhaps the terrible news from Margaret had my head in a weird place.

"I think this vacation is probably going to get cut short. I'm not very relaxed, so this is pointless. I need to get back and work on my marketing plan." I stomped off in the direction of the lake house.

"No, no. Let's give it a few more days. We both need to disengage from work. I'm guilty of it too, I know. Sorry."

"So, you want to take the boat out today then and step away from our phones?" I asked, fully expecting him to say no so that I could cut him loose and kick him to the curb. I'd had enough shit for today already.

"I'd love that. Raise the mast!" he said, swooping me in his grip and pulling me into him tight. "But first, I need my girl to shower with me. Come ride my salty seas."

I circled my arms around his neck and hung on, pushing my anger and confusion aside. It was early, and Margaret's confession had shaken me. My brain wasn't working correctly, and like usual, I'd probably done something to piss him off, justifying his douche-bag behavior today. If he'd forgiven me that easily, I could start over and forgive him too.

"Aye, aye, captain," I answered.

"Woohoo! Yar!" he shouted, skipping us down the road in a silly dance.

I broke out into giggles as he ran, carrying me up the hill and through the fog back home.

I sat on the back of the boat and folded my arms while Preston maneuvered us into the crowded cove. Seth and I'd argued the entire morning about whose turn it was to take the boat out until Fred and Margaret showed up to referee us into compliance. All it had taken was one pleading look on Margaret's tired face, and I'd lost whatever fight I had in me. I'd grown up with Dumb and Dumber. Another afternoon spent with the duo couldn't do much more harm.

Already, a dozen boats parked their anchors in the popular hangout spot nestled in between two rocky cliffs. A steady stream of music played from the massive three-story yacht in the center of the cove. Rows of lounge chairs lined the wooden deck on the highest level, where groups of gorgeous, exotic women were lying in the sun in bathing suits that served as practically nothing more than dental floss. A black flag with a golden etched M was perched atop the highest mast, whipping in the wind.

"That's Beaumont's boat. What's he doing here?" Jeff stiffened.

I popped the top on the tanning oil bottle and squeezed a small amount into my palm. The scent of coconut instantly lifted my mood—that and showing off my man's sculpted body. His washboard abs flexed as I rubbed the oil into his skin. He'd taken his shirt off as soon as he stepped into the boat. The sight of his oiled-up muscles caught everyone's eyes. Even Preston rolled his eyes before looking away and wrinkling his nose.

"You know him?" I asked, lowering my voice and rubbing the rest of the lotion on myself.

"Of course. He's a client ... and not a very good one," he growled. "He took me out on that thing once." He tipped his head toward the yacht. "Tried to woo me into a deal. But I could read between the lines, the wines, and the babes he threw at me."

"Babes?" Melanie asked, adjusting her top.

"Malcolm Beaumont is a really successful porn producer," Seth chimed in, kicking off his flip-flops.

"I see," Melanie said, raising her eyes to the top of the yacht and back down again as we pulled in right past it.

"This okay?" Preston asked, turning the engine off.

"Looks good." Seth rose from his seat and stabilized the boat, throwing the ladder over the side.

Melanie and I folded down the back seats and spread our towels across the scorching leather.

"I'm going to say hi. You know, business." Jeff dived off the tip of the boat and swam toward the yacht before I could protest.

"So much for you two getting a relaxing day on the water." Melanie elbowed me.

"Well, it's business. I get it. If I had any clients to network with here, I'd do it too." I followed Jeff with my eyes as he pulled himself up the yacht and into a crowd of hot bikini babes and mediocre middle-aged men.

I squinted at the bright sun reflecting off the water and pulled my cover-up over my head. I'd finally gotten the chance to wear my new bathing suit that I'd designed myself. It was a mixture of leopard print and gold with straps crisscrossing over my back.

"That is so cute! Where did you get it?" Melanie asked, reaching out to touch the silk-like fabric.

"I made it." I beamed. "I actually made it last year, but I've been too busy to use it or test it."

"Test it? Like, see if you can wear it all day and it's comfortable?" Melanie slipped her top off and stepped out of her shorts. Her bathing suit barely held in her overflowing chest.

"Test it ... like this." Preston came up behind me and put his arms around my waist, picking me up and throwing me overboard.

My ass hit the water with a thud. I dipped below the cool surface and paddled my way back up, gasping for breath as I reached air. I wiped my hair from my eyes.

"You fucker!" I shouted.

"I was helping you! Besides, you can't say you didn't expect it. It's a tradition." Preston backed away from the edge of the boat as I tore through the water like a shark.

"When we were fifteen! I'm not a kid anymore, jerkface. I know you can't grow up, but leave me the hell out of your crap!"

I pulled myself up the ladder and stomped over to him, jabbing my finger into his chest. His pecs tightened at my touch. I let my finger drift down, tracing the ridge of his muscles before I realized what I'd done.

He flinched at my touch, darting his eyes to my stiffened nipples peeking from under the thin fabric.

"I don't think it passed that test," he said.

I looked down at my breasts and my very apparent camel toe. I would have been dressed more modestly in a soggy, worn tissue.

"Fuck." I grabbed a towel and wrapped it around me, tucking the fabric tight.

A loud cheer came from the top deck of Malcolm's yacht. Four women had taken off their tops and tossed them to a boat of young men below. I scanned the nearby boats. Everyone had their phone out, filming the skeptical.

Preston glanced to the yacht and back to me.

"You can do that too. Take it off. Not like I haven't seen it before," Preston whispered, raking his eyes from my lips to my chest.

"Do you want me to throw you overboard?" I huffed.

"Depends. Can you toss me up there?" He jutted his chin out in the direction of the topless women.

I rolled my eyes.

"You can go hang out with Jeff." I turned away, sitting down beside Melanie and playing with my phone.

"Are you okay?" Seth nudged me. "You haven't seemed like yourself lately. You seem distracted."

"What's that supposed to mean?" My skin prickled.

"I'm going to go"—Melanie looked from side to side— "over there and get some water. Anyone want anything?" She pointed toward the cooler tucked under the steering wheel.

I shook my head.

She jumped to her feet and pulled Preston to the other side of the boat.

"I'm not trying to offend you. I've just noticed you've been acting differently, is all. If there's something wrong, you can tell me," Seth said.

"Did you know Margaret has cancer?" Cold droplets of water fell from my hair, dripping down my back and soaking my towel. An icy chill crept up my spine.

"What? Margaret as in Marg and Fred?" he asked.

"Yep."

"No! What the hell? No one told me." He leaned forward on his elbows and rubbed his palms across his face, as if he could scrub his fear away.

I glanced at Melanie and Preston at the other end of the boat. She was speaking to him with an animated expression, but I couldn't tell what they were discussing. The yacht's loud music drowned out their voices. Preston had taken his shirt off, revealing the only abs in sight that could compete with Jeff's. His shorts hung low on his tapered hips, exposing that devilish V muscle that led straight to a man's hot zone.

"She started treatment last week," I said, drawing my attention back to the yacht, where Jeff stood next to two topless women as they took selfies. I rubbed my stomach, trying to rid myself of the punch my boyfriend had delivered straight to my gut.

"Jeez. I had no idea. Fuck. I hope she's all right." Seth rubbed the back of his neck before following my gaze. "That's not the only thing bothering you, is it?"

"Oh. You mean, my man up there with those porn stars? Nah. That doesn't bother me at all. It's just business," I spit out my excuse like venom. The lie burned in my mouth.

"Business like the kind Dad used to do on his business trips?"

"I'd know it if it was funny business," I snapped.

"Would you? Do you think that's healthy up there? I'd never do that to Melanie. Talk about a slap in the face." Seth rubbed his jawline and looked away from the shameful spectacle atop the yacht.

Preston and Melanie both watched as my boyfriend posed with porn stars. He was leaning down, sticking his face right between two sets of ginormous and perfectly round breasts. Even my fake ones by Fork's most famous plastic surgeon couldn't compare with these Beverly Hills boobs. My entire body flushed in raging heat.

"Mingling with clients is a good business decision. Mom would tell me to let it go and focus on Minx. Let him do his thing. I don't need him." I swallowed the lie and the knot forming in my throat.

"And how many men has Mom blasted through? And she's still not happy. She's lonely. She can pretend all she wants that she's this powerhouse boss babe. But at the end of the day, she pours herself a glass or three of wine and flips through old photos on her phone." He sighed, nodding toward my phone in my hand.

"She's not lonely!" I said, turning my phone off and setting it beside me.

"She is. And it took me moving far away to understand it and learn what a healthy relationship looked like. The shit we saw with Mom and Dad, and Mom and all the other men? That wasn't healthy. It fucked me up, and it fucked you up too. Your boyfriend is up there, mingling with topless babes, and you're down here, upset about Margaret. That's not okay. He should be here with you." A sharp look of concern spread across his face, bringing his brows together. He looked so much like our mom.

"How do you know about healthy relationships? You aren't exactly the poster child for relationship advice," I scoffed and brought my legs up under me, scooting and situating my wet back onto dry leather.

"No. But I met someone who's patient and teaching me. She's not an entrepreneur or an executive badass. She's a nurse, and she's opened me up to more in life than Mom ever taught me," he said.

"That's because you're a guy. You didn't have to struggle with rising to the top. Mom was much harder on me," I protested.

"She was by no means easy on me."

I looked away, avoiding the bullshit on the yacht and the bullshit conversation that was slowly making me more and more uncomfortable.

"Look, I'm just saying … you aren't the same. The last few days, you've been acting strange. I care, okay?" He lowered his voice.

I slumped my shoulders forward and let out a long sigh. "I haven't felt like myself either. I feel like I'm in a fog. I'm not sure what it is. Margaret, Jeff, your asshole friend Preston. Work, Mom. I miss Hailey. Who knows? Things were great back home, but now, all of a sudden, Jeff and I are fighting. And I'm not even sure why."

I quickly flicked my eyes back to my boyfriend. Jeff waved good-bye to the girls and dived headfirst into the water with barely a splash. The topless babes watched as he swam his way back to our boat and heaved himself up over the side. He had muscles on top of muscles, flexing on even more muscles. I couldn't tear my eyes from him either.

"Sorry about that. I had to say hi. Got a meeting next week for a new contract out of those few minutes though." Jeff grabbed a towel and dried himself. He tousled his hair with his hand, flinging droplets of water around him.

"Looks like you got more than that," I muttered.

"If you want," he whispered in my ear, leaning down, "we can do the third thing again tonight. Or four even. There were a few women up there definitely putting out feelers."

I stared straight past Jeff and into Preston's eyes. He shook his head and turned away, as if he'd heard Jeff's proposal.

"Actually, I don't feel so well. You can stay." I waved him away. "Think you can take me home, Preston?" I shouted to the other side of the boat.

Preston pulled the keys from his pocket and was at the steering wheel in an instant. Seth and Melanie exchanged worried glances.

"Well?" I eyed Jeff, who stood, glancing over his shoulder, back toward the yacht.

"I'll go. I've got work to do anyway," he said, stretching his arms overhead and yawning.

Preston slammed his foot on the gas, sending Jeff tumbling to the floor. His legs flipped over his head, and his butt stuck straight into the air before he crashed back down again.

"Sorry! Fuck. This thing's out of gear!" Preston said, cringing and putting his hands in the air, as if he were being held hostage.

"Are you okay?" I asked, stooping to help Jeff to his feet.

Jeff pulled his shoulder from my grip and nodded. "Of course I'm okay. Guess I'd better wear a seat belt if this dipshit is driving."

Preston peered at me from behind Jeff, caught my eye, and winked.

I waited until Jeff wasn't looking and returned Preston's wink with a smirk.

$\mathcal{S}ix$

PRESTON

I wasn't one to save a princess or stomp out a dumpster fire. But after watching the way Jeff had worked those thot porn stars on old man Beaumont's yacht, I could smell a rat. He'd used the same moves I had with women but worse—he'd used them directly in front of his girl. Even I didn't have the lack of class to do that. If anyone was going to be an asshat to Madison Sheffield, it was going to be me. But telling Madison her boyfriend was a grade-A douche canoe wouldn't go over well. She'd roll her eyes and not believe a word I told her. I had to do something to prove it.

Enter my favorite tool for a tool—muskrat lure straight from a muskrat's butthole. Or so I'd heard. Like I said, I could smell a rat, and pretty soon, everyone in the lake house would be able to smell him too. I'd always had my suspicions about Jeff. But seeing him slowly break Madison with that bullshit at the firepit or the bullshit on the boat was the last straw. She was a brat, but she didn't deserve to be reduced to his toy that he could push around. I pulled the bottle from my suitcase and unwrapped it from the swaddling of bubble wrap.

"Dude, why the hell are you traveling with muskrat piss?" Seth asked while sitting on the edge of the bed.

"It's not piss. It's from their butt glands. And I have it because I planned on playing a joke on you. But I've got bigger fish to fry. Or rats to slay."

I loosened the cap on the bottle and brought it to my nose before gagging. An acidic taste rose in the back of my throat, and the memories of firepit night came flooding back into my brain. I shook my head and focused back on the task at hand.

"Smell," I said, sticking the bottle under his nostrils.

"Fuck, bro! Why would you do that to me?" He fake retched over the side of the bed.

"I wasn't going to put it on you! I was going to put it around the place outside and suggest you two have a romantic night under the stars, tossing about with some muskrat love." I laughed. "It seemed much better in my head. Besides, when I saw the name on the bottle, I couldn't resist. I knew it would come in handy one day."

I screwed the cap back on and read the bottle aloud, "*Stink Stuff: Muskrat Lure.*"

"Guess that's one way to get some beaver. Are you ever going to grow up?" he asked.

"Probably not."

"Figures."

"I don't have a reason to." I shrugged.

Seth flicked his head, tossing his hair out of his face. Since I'd seen him last, his skin looked brighter, his demeanor had become softer, and his eyes had that simp-like dewiness to them. He was pussy-whipped to the tenth degree.

"You're about to graduate. You'll have to be an adult then. And … maybe get a wife," he said.

The bottle fell from my grip, landing on the blankets scattered on my unkempt bed. I never understood the process of making a bed when, in a few hours, I'd crawl right back into it.

"What? Is your girlfriend a witch? Did she cast some sort of spell on you? This whole *new you* bullshit is a bromance killer, man. We used to guzzle beer and ogle tits. Now, it's all on me to carry the tradition, and I'm worn out! I already get enough drama from my mom. Now you?" I threw my hands in the air and walked toward the window, staring outside toward the lake.

Jeff and Madison were swinging in the hammock underneath a pergola by the water. She rested her head on his chest while he played with his phone.

"I still guzzle beer and ogle tits. It's just one pair of tits. And for me, it's the best pair of tits in the world. You know that high we got from banging chicks all the time? Being in love is like that, except much, much better. It's on another level. I can't explain it."

I blew a loud breath out of my nose and shut the blinds.

"I'll take your word for it. Come on. Let's put a few drops of that butt juice on Jeff's deodorant before they come back inside."

"Why are we doing this anyway? I thought you hated my sister?" He picked up the bottle of lure and dangled it in front of my face with a smirk.

"I do."

"So, why are you trying to protect her from that asshole?"

"I'm not." I grabbed the lure and squeezed it in my palm.

"Bullshit."

"No, I'm not saving her. I'm just fucking with him. I know his type. People like him get away with too much bullshit. Hell, I'm damn near like him, except I'm not. I wouldn't have pulled the yacht shit he did. I think that was the first time I've seen Madison tear up. It was scary. Fuck.

Why do you have me getting deep? What's wrong with you?"

"Me. I'm what's wrong with him." Melanie stomped over to the bed and plopped herself down across the wrinkled sheets. "I heard every bit of that conversation. And it's not because I was passing by. It's because I was eavesdropping. Hmmph." She pressed her lips together and stared at me, daring me to protest.

"I didn't mean it like that." I shrank back, stepping away from my best friend and his bulldog.

She held out her hand and pressed her thumb to her fingers, signaling for me to shut up. "Zip it and listen up, you two nimrods," she continued. "We need a plan. Preston's right. Jeff's not good for her. He's a narcissistic asshole. I've dated my fair share of them. I knew it the second he laughed about her falling in spin class. Those men are all charm on the outside but snakes just below the surface. Unlike this asshole right here, who's purely a douche bag through and through."

She tossed a glance in my direction. I nodded in agreement.

Seth rubbed his hands together. "All right. Let's save my bratty little sister from the big, bad wolf. You know if we run him away, she's likely to kill us all in our sleep, right?"

"I have tranquilizers in the car if things get rough." Melanie pointed her finger in the air.

I blinked back a rush of emotion, suddenly in approval of Seth's choice of chicks.

"Let's do it. Anywhere you want to dab this besides his deodorant?" I uncurled the bottle from my palm.

"Deodorant? We're mixing it with that expensive cologne of his. Lawdy, it's been giving me a headache anyway. I think I'd rather smell this ass juice." Melanie snatched the bottle of Stink Stuff from my hand.

I exchanged grins with Seth. I was okay with a bromance, plus one. For now anyway. But that doe-eyed love shit would never work on me. Even if I could find someone as amazing as Melanie, I wasn't forever signing my dick away to one woman. There was plenty of "The P" to go around.

The next morning, I bumped into Fred, who had just come inside from weeding the garden. He'd been outside since dawn, well before the sun scorched overhead. His long, drawn face sagged behind tired eyes, like he hadn't slept in months. I knew the look. My dad had worn the same expression until my mother's cancer was all clear. When Seth had told me about Margaret, I felt that dread all over again.

"How's the chemo treating her so far?" I asked as I rummaged through the shelves for two coffee mugs.

"It's slowed her down. You know Marg. She usually can't sit still. But her energy is zapped and her mood with it. I'm afraid she'll get so down that she'll give up fighting. Did your mom go through a depression like that?" He sat down at the breakfast table with an old-man groan.

"She did. But Margaret helped, honestly. And everyone else who kept sending her well wishes and pushing her on. I don't think we left her alone long enough for her to think about her situation. We kept her as busy as we could. My dad used quick getaways, lots of dates, and special surprises to keep her on her toes. Someone sat with her through every treatment." I poured coffee grinds into the coffee machine's filter and pressed the brew button.

"You're a good son, Preston. Your mother is lucky to have you. I wish my children were closer. If Marg leaves this world before me, I'll be forever alone. How do you do it?"

"Do what?"

A steady stream of coffee poured from the spout into the glass kettle, filling it with my favorite dark roast.

Anytime I was in town, Marg stocked the pantry with my favorite things—coffee, beer, protein powder, and beef jerky.

"Stay alone. You're what, mid-twenties now? Don't you want someone? Doesn't it get lonely? Don't you want kids? Who'll take care of you when you're old?"

I leaned back into the counter, folding my arms across my chest and stretching my legs out in front of me.

"Have you been talking to my mom?" I asked.

"Just a little." He smiled.

"Go figure." I pushed my back off the counter and filled our mugs before carrying them to the table and sitting down.

"She's been talking to Marg a lot lately. Says she's worried about you," he said, reaching for the sugar and creamer.

"Worried? Why?" I brought the piping hot black liquid to my lips and breathed in the steam. The deliciously bitter taste lingered on my tongue well after I took the first sip.

"She wishes you could find someone special too. She thinks all this malarky about you liking being alone is just your tough exterior and you learned that from your dad, unfortunately. He had problems showing emotion, too, until she got ahold of him." He tapped the wiry whiskers on his chin. "He allows himself to be vulnerable. Yeah! That was the word she used."

"It's too early for this. I never thought you'd be conspiring with my mom against me."

"Don't think of it as conspiring. Except, well, maybe Marg and I were a little last night. What we think you need is someone who can match your bullheadedness. That's why you haven't settled. No one challenges you. They just fall into your lap. You need someone just as stubborn as you are."

"Sure, sure. That's it. It's not the fact that I like having my choice of women and my freedom." I mentally scrolled my little black book, taking note of anyone who might meet me at my level of stubbornness. No one even came close.

"Well, well, well. Look what the cat dragged in early this morning." Madison skipped past me in her sports bra and running shorts and stuck her tongue out. "And good morning to you, Fred. Not sure why you'd want to wake up with this dolt. But I'm glad you're here!" She patted him on the back before opening a cabinet. The ridge on her abs flexed as she reached for a mug and poured herself a coffee.

"Mornin', Madison. You've not changed a bit! Still got that spark in ya, I reckon. Just like your mama." Fred slurped his coffee.

I caught a whiff of the familiar putrid scent drifting toward me before I saw him make his grand entrance.

"Good morning, everyone!" Jeff bellowed, coming up behind Madison and putting his arms around her waist.

"What the hell is that smell?" She turned on her heels and pushed him away. A look of disgust crossed her face.

"You smell that too? I thought I was just smelling things. I think it's my cologne. Maybe it's spoiled. It's designer, and it cost almost as much as my mortgage. I bet I didn't store it right!" He pulled his collar from his neck and lifted it to his nose, taking a deep breath.

"You smell like a dead animal inside another dead animal inside of a human corpse that was left in the sun for two weeks, shriveled into a rotted raisin, and then grew mold. Fuck!" She gagged, covered her mouth, and shifted her eyes back to Fred. "I mean, frick! I'm sorry."

"You're excused on that one. I've only smelled something like that once before, and it was in the woods and covered in shit." Fred's thin lips parted into a grimace.

I stuck my nose into my mug and took a long drink.

"Go shower! I can't run with you like that." She shooed him back upstairs before dumping a massive load of sugar and creamer into her coffee and taking a picture of it for her social media.

"What's wrong, Madison? I thought you were tough. Can't you put up with a little spoiled musk on your man? Weak." I waved my hands in the air, trying to clear Jeff's funk.

"This was your doing, wasn't it?" She stirred a spoon in her mug, scraping it hard against the bottom.

I rubbed the grin from my mouth and looked away. "No idea what you're talking about. I think he just left his cologne out to rot. That's all."

"I don't care if he smells like the inside of a beaver's asshole; he's mine, and I'll still … I'll still …" She rolled her eyes up into her hairline and tapped her foot. "I'll still like him more than anyone will ever like an annoying asshat like you!"

She stomped out of the kitchen. I followed her with my gaze, lingering a bit too long on her firm thighs.

"Oh my." Fred chuckled.

"It was muskrat lure. Good one, eh?" I laughed.

"Jeez, boy. That's terrible. But that's not what I'm amused over. That girl right there, Madison, she's as bullheaded as you. She's your Margaret. She's your Melanie. Hell, her name even starts with an *M*. All the signs point to her. You catch her—with something other than stink bait—and you'll be as happy as a pig in shit."

"What? No way! We hate each other." The smile faded from my face.

"I don't see hate. I see untapped chemistry. Better get that Jeff out and weasel your way in. Or muskrat your way in. Whatever." He finished his coffee with an audible sigh and rose to his feet. "Good luck getting rid of him. But better save the luck for bagging Madison, especially since she's just like her mama. You can't tame it. But you can roll with it. Margaret had a bit of that spitfire in her too. It's fun while it lasts."

I picked up my phone and began to dial my mom once Fred left, but the sound of an air horn, followed by a string of curses and my name, blasted down the stairs. Madison had finally sat on my rigged toilet. I quickly shoved my phone in my pocket, ran outside, and disappeared into a thick layer of fog.

My feet hit the pavement hard as I ran down the street and far away from the truths Fred just spouted. The only woman who popped in my brain when I scrolled my mental black book for a challenge was Madison. She'd taken me like a champ and given it right back. I'd never thought of dating my best friend's sister. But Fred was right. My grade-A douche-bag tendencies matched her grade-A bratty ones. We were perfect together, except for the hatred we harbored for each other.

I jogged across the wet pavement until the lake house was no longer in view while letting Madison overtake my thoughts. I remembered her when she had been thirteen, sketching on her notepad down by the lake. Her long hair trailed down her back and whipped in the air. She turned and looked at me with a sneer, stopping me in my tracks. I'd been on my way to ask if she wanted to go out in the boat. Seth had to study, and I had no one. But the look on her face had sent me right back up to my room.

I thought of the time she'd gotten food poisoning from the oysters I'd dared her to order when her family took us out to celebrate her high school graduation. She spent the entire weekend on the cold tiled bathroom floor in delirium. I sat on the other side of the door, letting her curse me for hours until she finally fell asleep. Only then had I walked away.

I remembered the time she'd shown up at my house after my mom's diagnosis. She brought over a badass basket, as she called it. She'd made it herself. It was pink and full of positive mantras, cozy robes, socks, meds for nausea, books, and snacks. And of course, it had the Sheffield flair to it, complete with boujee fur and gold trimmings. My mom talked about that basket for weeks. But when I'd tried to approach Madison to thank her, she'd flipped her hair and bounced away.

But my favorite memory was no doubt the newest. When I had ridden her ass like a rock star and she'd turned her head, locking eyes on me instead of Jeff. That did it. I'd felt a fluttering in my stomach that I thought was pre-orgasm jitters. But now, I knew I had been mistaken. That tingling was those bullshit butterflies I'd heard pussies talk about. I'd thought I was immune to them.

I paused, leaning on my knees to catch my breath. My heart pounded in my chest in a way I'd not felt before. I wasn't out of breath from running. I was fit as fuck. I was out of breath from the sudden realization that I didn't hate Madison. She hated me.

"Shit," I murmured, staring up into the sky. "Shit. Shit. Shit!"

"That's what you are, loser! Ha-ha!" Madison yelled, blasting through the fog and right past me in a series of whoops and jumps. Her long white hair flowed out behind her like a veil. A fucking wedding veil.

I staggered to the side of the road and watched her disappear. I was in love with my worst enemy and my best friend's sister.

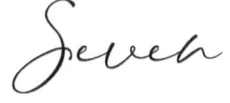

MADISON

Jeff had scrubbed himself raw all morning, and he still smelled like death. Every time he crossed my path, I graciously excused myself to another room, so I could gag. Whatever asshole stunt Preston had pulled worked. Which meant I had to go bigger. It was one thing to play a prank on me. But messing with my man brought the game to a whole other level.

Lucky for Preston, I kept his secret trick to myself. Otherwise, I'd have to scrape him off the pavement once my man beast finished him. I knew how rough Jeff could be in bed. I couldn't imagine the ass-kickings he was capable of giving on the streets. One wrong move, and he'd give Preston the punishment he deserved.

In a way, I wasn't too pissed about the smell of ass lingering on Jeff. It would at least keep the porn stars at bay. Just last night, I'd seen they'd posted their topless selfies and tagged him in their photos. He'd responded with winking emojis and probably a slide into their DMs.

While he scrubbed himself raw, I decided to sneak into his phone. But it was useless. His face was his password, and no matter how much I tried to give it a smoldering, chiseled jawline look, I couldn't pass for Jeff. I'd either have to learn to trust him or do my own thing and ignore the suspect feelings I had.

I sat at the vanity, picking my peeling orange skin off in flakes. My fake tan had finally begun to fade in big, dry patches. I looked worse now than I had before.

"Princess," Jeff said, emerging from the bathroom in only a towel and kissing the top of my head.

I caught a faint whiff of death and bit back a cringe.

"All better?" I lifted my gaze to him.

His thick golden hair dripped water down the sides of his freshly shaved jaw.

"Much." He tapped his fingertip against my forehead. "You've got a pimple," he pointed out before walking away.

"Um ... correct. I can see that for myself. You don't have to point out my flaws." I picked up my hairbrush and pulled the long white strands from it before stuffing them in the trash bin beside me.

He held up his hands in defense. "Whoa. You don't have to overreact! I just thought you might like to know in case you wanted to fix it before dinner. I know how you are."

"How am I?"

"Picky."

I busied myself with my hair and kept my mouth shut. I didn't have the energy to argue, let alone prove him wrong. He wasn't. I was picky as hell. I'd spotted the pimple first thing this morning and been rigorously applying treatment to it on and off all day. But it was still there, like a thorn in my side. Similar to how I'd been feeling about Jeff these last few days.

"What time do you leave tomorrow?" I asked.

"I called for a ride to pick me up at nine. That way, I can have the day to gather myself before heading back into meetings. These assholes I have scheduled for tomorrow will try to pull one over on me. I know it. Heh." He snorted. "They have no idea who they're dealing with. I didn't get this far in business by playing nice."

"That's unfortunately the way it works." I set my brush down and applied a thin layer of moisturizer over my face.

"Aren't you smart?" he said.

"Duh. Where have you been?" I smirked at his reflection in the mirror. Drops of water clung to the ridges of his pecs.

"Focusing on that ass instead of that brain. Come over here." He dropped his towel and kicked it to the side. His dick sprang up like a cannon.

I hesitated, hoping he hadn't sprayed his eau de ass cologne down his pants.

"Madison?" Melanie knocked at the door. Her voice sounded hurried.

"Be right there!" I called, stooping to pick up Jeff's towel and throwing it back to him.

Jeff rolled his eyes as I cracked open the door and slid out.

"What's up?" My voice trailed off into a whisper when I caught the look of dread on her face.

"It's Margaret. She had a bad reaction to this round. She … momentarily stopped breathing. Fred's with her, but we're going to go see her, and I was—" she started.

"I'll grab my bag." I held up a finger and disappeared back into my bedroom.

"Everything okay?" Jeff shimmied into his pants, pulling them up and over his perky butt.

For once, I didn't feel disappointed that I was missing a rendezvous in bed with him.

"Margaret's in the hospital. She had a bad reaction to chemo. I'm going to run up there. Will you come?"

"Oh." He lowered his eyes. "I don't do well around those things, babe."

"You'd be doing it for me though. I don't want to be alone up there. She needs someone, and her family is way the fuck on the other side of the coast."

"What about George?"

"You mean, Fred?"

"Yeah, Fred."

"Of course he's there. It's what partners do!" I huffed, throwing my hair up into a messy bun.

"I wouldn't be comfortable. I'm sorry. I'll be here when you get back. I can get some work done while you're gone."

"But this is me reaching out. And your response is like a slap in the face. You've hidden your true colors for so long, but now, I see them clear as day."

"I said, no." He raised his voice, slamming his fist onto the dresser. My collection of perfume bottles rattled.

I sucked in my breath and stepped back.

"What the fuck is going on in here? I can hear you two from downstairs!" Seth pushed open the door, followed by Melanie.

"Nothing. He was just leaving." I jerked my head in Jeff's direction.

"I'm leaving?" Jeff asked.

"Yeah, you're leaving." I reached for his suitcase and threw it on the bed, spilling the contents out.

"We'll be downstairs, waiting on you, Madison. Jeff, I'll call you a ride." Melanie pulled Seth away and shut the door.

"Are you breaking up with me because I won't go see some old lady I don't even know dying in a hospital?" he said in an icy shrill. His pupils dilated, almost turning his eyes entirely black.

"Get the fuck out before I have you removed." I grabbed my phone from the nightstand and waited as he packed his things, throwing them into his suitcase.

"You're batshit crazy! A damn lunatic. All of you women, you just aren't worth it." He shook his head and zipped up his luggage.

I bit my tongue to keep from fighting back. There wasn't any winning with Jeff. He could think I was batshit crazy and maybe even convince me I was, but I wouldn't fall into the trap of arguing with him. I'd never win. I'd seen him use this manipulation tactic on conference calls. When a client had had an issue once, he'd turned it around and blamed them. They'd hung up, accepting his failure as theirs.

"I don't know what happened to you. But I'm sorry if I hurt you in some way." He sniffled with the fakest crocodile tears I'd ever seen. "Bye, Madison."

He grabbed his suitcase and shuffled downstairs. I didn't emerge from my bedroom until his ride arrived. I peeked out of the window and watched him leave, unable to move until I knew he was gone for good. Then, I collapsed onto the floor and let myself cry.

Melanie stuck her head in my door while knocking.

"Want to talk?" she asked.

"Not really. Let's just go see Margaret, okay?" I wiped my face with the back of my hand and rose to my feet.

"Come on. Preston's already there. He's been sitting with her all morning. Maybe we can relieve him a bit." She hooked her arm around mine and squeezed me.

"Preston? The asswad Preston?"

"Yep. That one." She laughed.

"I've never been so confused in my life as I am today."

"Aw, honey. It's part of growing up. Throughout your life, people are going to come and go. Surprise you, change you, scare you, love you. I'd tell you that you'll figure it out one day, but you won't. None of us do. Keeps things interesting, I guess," she said.

I paused and turned toward her, noticing her eyes were as wet as mine.

"I'm happy Seth met you. You're good for him."

"Thank you. I'm happy I met both of you." She pulled me in for a hug.

I swallowed my earlier encounter with Jeff, pushed it deep down into the pits of my soul, and held my head up high.

It would take a lot more than a psycho ex-lover to break me.

I spent the evening in the hospital waiting room, sandwiched in between Preston and Seth. Only two of us were allowed inside Margaret's room at a time, and since Melanie knew nursing lingo, she stayed with Fred to translate the doctor's orders. Meanwhile, I had to put up with two dumbasses while carrying on a text war with Jeff.

Jeff: Can we talk?

Me: No.

Jeff: I'm really sorry. I should have just gone up there with you. I have a hard time dealing with deep stuff like that. I wish her the best though.

My fingers flew across the phone in sharp taps.

Me: Stop texting me. We're done.

"You aren't mad, are ya, Maddie?" Preston peered over my shoulder, sneaking a peek at my phone.

I tilted it away from his view and hissed.

"Dude. Don't." Seth shook his head.

"Why? Where's your douche boyfriend anyway?" Preston stretched his legs out in front of him and yawned.

His shiny leather shoes reflected the blinding fluorescent lights overhead. I'd noticed his stylish shoes at breakfast. But paying a compliment to Preston would make me sick. I'd need to gag the words out of my throat to make him feel special.

A television in the corner of the room blared the evening news, drowning out the low murmur of voices in the waiting room. An older man tucked a newspaper under his armpit and shuffled toward us, settling in front of our chairs.

"He's back home. We're through." I cleared my throat and rechecked my phone.

> *Jeff: It doesn't have to be like that. Why are you being so mean to me? I only want to talk.*

I shivered in my seat as the air conditioner kicked on overhead and blasted a chill right down my blouse.

> *Me: I can't do this anymore. I thought things were different, but our personalities are too conflicting.*

"What? How? Why? It's because the thot yacht, isn't it?" Preston asked, flicking a strand of hair from his face.

"The what?" Seth scratched his head.

"Old man Beaumont's yacht. That's what he calls it. I've been on it once before, and let me tell you … what happens on that boat stays on that boat. Unless, of course, he records it for all the world to see, makes millions on it, and then calls it a day. You know, a typical day for a porn gangster." Preston sighed.

"Did someone say porn?" The old man peered over his newspaper and raised his eyebrows.

"Ugh. No." I shook my head and nudged Preston with my elbow.

A visitor holding a bouquet arrived through the automatic glass doors and walked straight past the nurses' station before disappearing down the hall in a hurry. The nurses hadn't bothered to look up from their screens.

"So, this thot yacht, what did you see happen on it?" Seth leaned sideways, inching closer to Preston and lowering his voice.

"Everything you could imagine." Preston held his hands out from his chest like he was groping a pair of massive boobs.

"Lucky," Seth said.

I switched my phone off and stashed it in my purse. "It's not because of the thot yacht. I don't want to talk about it. I need to think happy thoughts. I need a distraction."

"Well, well, well. Aren't you in the right hands?" Preston rubbed his palms together.

"Great," I said. "Let's forget I said that. I just want to go see Margaret, and then I think I'm ready to go home." I scuffed my shoe on the floor, leaving a black mark smudged across the linoleum. "Wish they'd let us in there."

"We can pass the time with a game. Get your mind off drama. Preston 'The P' to the rescue!" Preston flexed his biceps and made his pecs dance under his thin top.

I rolled my eyes. "Sure, sure. Because you're a white knight. You're the jester or the fool … or the tool," I mused.

"You don't give me any credit," Preston said, turning his face toward the television.

"Why should I?" I asked.

"Can you two not argue for one moment? Jeez. You're like an old married couple!" Seth pushed himself out of the dingy chair and made his way to the vending machine.

"I was trying to help you, Madison. I know you liked that dude. Sorry you're upset," Preston said.

"I shouldn't have snapped at you like that. Thanks for trying to help. Though you've never done that before. Are you feeling okay? Do I need to check you into this hospital?" I put the back of my hand to his forehead.

His lips parted in a grin. "Yep. I'm all gravy, baby. You know, my mom used to come here for treatment. There's a vacant floor up top. I only know because I was banging a dirty nurse back then. But that's beside the point. Let's go up there and have some fun."

A rush of heat shot between my thighs. I could use anything to take my mind off of Jeff. The best relationship advice I'd ever heard was also the most scandalous—to get over someone, I needed to get under someone else. I never really had anyone to get over, but at this point, I'd try anything even if that meant banging my brother's douche-bag best friend.

"Here." Seth tossed a bag of chips to Jeff and one to me. "I could tell you two were getting hangry."

Preston's arm brushed against mine, sending the hairs on the back of my neck standing on end. He licked his lips before opening the bag of chips.

"Thanks, bro. I was just telling Madison we could go upstairs and get into some shenanigans. You up for it?" Preston tipped the bag into his mouth and shoveled the chips down.

"What?" I tossed the bag of chips back to Seth. My white leggings and my hips weren't a match for the bag of flaming hot cheese balls.

"He said he wanted a threesome upstairs!" The old man peeked over his newspaper again and wiggled his brows.

"No! No. What the fuck?" Preston wiped the crumbs from his mouth. "Shenanigans. As in pranks and shit."

The man shrugged and disappeared behind his paper again.

I crossed my legs and sighed. Maybe I needed to be checked into the hospital for entertaining the idea of fucking Preston. Especially when the only thing on his mind was juvenile behavior.

"I'm down. Lead the way," Seth said.

Preston gripped the armrests and pushed himself up, flexing his biceps in my face.

"Come on." He wiped his palms on his pants and reached for my hand.

I grabbed his greasy fingers and let him whisk me away.

We strolled past the inattentive nurses and rode the mirrored elevator to the top.

"Ever done it in one of these things?" Seth scratched his head, wiggling his hips to his reflection in the mirror. "Melanie wants more excitement. I need some ideas."

"I did! This same one, to be exact." Preston patted the back mirror, where an advertisement for depression meds hung lopsided.

The elevator slowed to a stop and parted its doors, revealing an abandoned hallway. Balls of dust and debris littered the floor, rolling like tumbleweeds from the draft of our steps.

"This is creepy." I took my phone out of my purse and snapped a couple of selfies.

"Do you ever put that damn thing away and just enjoy the moment?" Seth asked. His voice echoed off the walls.

"I'm documenting in case the ghost of a mental ward patient decides to slit my throat and run off with my killer heels." I climbed atop an unkempt cot and propped up my feet, snapping a picture of my black heels against the faded cream hospital bed. The Exit sign blinked in the background.

"Let's have some fun." Seth jumped atop the bed and nudged me off. "Push me, Preston. Let's see how fast this thing goes."

Preston grabbed the rails and barreled down the hallway, shoving the bed hard before letting go. Seth threw his head back and laughed while spinning sideways into a corner and stopping in a crash. He stuck his hand between his legs and hobbled off the cot.

"I gotta fucking piss." Seth ran down the hall, scanning the signs on the wall. He pushed against a swinging door and disappeared.

"Wanna play?" Preston inched closer to me. His gaze dropped from my face to my breasts.

I took two long strides to him and whispered, "Bring it."

He let out a grunt and swept me off my heels.

"I forgot. You like it rough." He tossed me on the bed behind him.

"Don't lie. You'll never forget that night." I sat up on my hands and knees, swaying my hips in the air.

"Cocktease." He bit his lip and reached out, grabbing my chin between the crook of his thumb and finger. "I've got something to stick into that bratty mouth of yours."

My nipples stiffened under my blouse as he whisked me into a maelstrom of raw sexual energy. I hadn't even felt this needy with Jeff. But something about the way Preston teased me was much less annoying and much more pleasurable.

"I thought we were racing," Seth said, jogging back to us.

Preston stepped away from me and cleared his throat. "We need a fourth to race."

"Yoo-hoo." The old man stuck his head out of the elevator and stepped across the threshold.

"Crap. It's the creepy old dude!" I whispered.

Preston and Seth stared at each other and giggled.

"What do we do?" Seth asked.

"If you think you can handle us, then come on, old man." Preston motioned for the man to get on another bed.

"Who're you calling old, sucker?" The man threw his newspaper to the ground and pushed himself off his heels, running until he collided with the cot. He stooped over, resting his upper half across the bed. "Shit," he groaned. "Damn it. You'll learn with age that sometimes, when you tell your body to do something, it takes it a while. In this case, it was a jump. Instead, these old bones said nah."

"I thought you said you weren't old." Preston smiled, helping the man onto the cot.

His bald head reflected the neon-red Exit sign.

"What? I don't remember. Not even sure how I got up here, sonny. Let's roll!" He bounced on the bed with a wince.

"Are you sure this is safe?" Seth said out of the corner of his mouth.

"No. But why not?" Preston said.

He grabbed the railing on the old man's cot and backed down the hall. Seth followed, rolling me into line beside the man. I studied his hunched profile and decided that he wasn't anything to worry about. If anything, he needed to worry about us.

"You're going down, honey!" he shouted.

"In your dreams!" I shouted back.

"One. Two. Three. Go!" Seth said, barreling my bed toward the end of the hall.

I glanced to my left and saw the look of determination on both the old man's and Preston's faces. It was like looking into the future. If I hadn't known Preston's family, I'd have thought this creepy guy was his dad.

The man roared and cracked an invisible whip in the air as he flew past us. Preston tried to dig his heels into the ground and stop the bed from crashing into the wall, but it was no use. The bed slammed into the brick anyway.

"Woowee! That was a tingle in the pants. Thankfully, I got them adult diapers on!" The man patted his butt.

"Ew!" I wrinkled my nose as Seth pushed our bed back into position.

"What else is there to do up here?" Seth asked.

"One of those beds with the stirrups." Preston raised his eyebrows and shot me a devilish smirk.

"Nope." I hopped to the floor and dusted off whatever disgusting bacteria particles clung to my new outfit.

"There's an old PA system." The old man perked up, crawled off the cot, and made his way toward a desk.

"What're we going to do with an intercom?" I folded my arms across my chest and followed behind him.

"This," he said as he pulled the microphone from its place and pushed a button. He held the speaker to his butt and farted. A loud and ridiculously long vibration rang throughout the hall.

Seth and Preston doubled over in laughter.

"That was the most disgusting thing I've ever seen. You're a dirty old man. You know that, right?" I pursed my lips and shook my head.

He beamed back at me. "When you ain't got nothing worth living for anymore, you run out of care. Here, you try!" He handed me the mic.

"I'm not farting into a microphone!" I threw my hands in the air.

"No. Not fart! Just say something funny." He shoved the microphone in my face, and I batted it away.

"I'm not putting my mouth anywhere near where you just had your droopy drawers. What the hell?!" I backed away, bumping into Preston.

"Come on, Madison. Where's your sense of fun? Watch this." Preston grabbed the microphone and shook it, seemingly shaking off any invisible farticles clinging to the mouthpiece.

"Seth Sheffield needs a sponge bath on floor two, level B. I repeat, Seth Sheffield needs a sponge bath on floor two, level B. Please be aware that this patient has a bad case of blue-ball-itis. Do not be alarmed at the swelling and abnormal color of his wrinkled sack. His girlfriend, a nurse, will drain it soon." Preston switched the button off on the mic, opened his palm, and let it fall to the desk.

Seth's jaw dropped. "She's going to kill me."

"Oh! Oh! I got one!" The old man bounced on his heels and swiped the microphone off the counter.

"Drop it, Mr. Goldren." A burly security guard stepped out of the elevator and made his way toward us.

"Harold." Mr. Goldren's shoulders slumped forward, stooping him even lower. "He always kills the mood."

"Are you three responsible for this man's shenanigans?" Harold asked, eyeing Seth, Preston, and me.

Preston put his hands in the air. "I'm innocent. It was these three."

"Oh, come on!" I said, blowing out a breath.

"Mmhmm. Well, let's go. I don't know why you three are here but don't come back today. Or for a while. And, you"—he pointed his finger at Mr. Goldren—"not a day before next Saturday. You hear?"

Mr. Goldren nodded and shuffled his feet toward the elevator.

We followed and rode down to the first floor in silence. Melanie was waiting when the doors opened.

"Seth!" she shrieked, grabbing his elbow and scolding him.

The old man laughed before turning to Preston and me. "Thanks. I needed that. She was here. First time I've felt her that strong in ages." He dipped his head and left, slowly creeping toward the entry.

"What was that all about?" I asked Harold.

"That's just Mr. Goldren. He comes here every Saturday evening. His wife used to work here, but she passed some years ago. Back when she was alive, he'd spend his Saturdays here so that he could be close to her when she worked weekends. Those two were like nothing I've ever seen. Prank war champions. Never a dull moment when they were around. But his dementia is getting worse. He'll be a patient here soon enough. Maybe he can finally rest then." Harold turned to leave.

I swallowed hard.

"Wow. Harold does kill the mood." Preston turned his watery gaze away.

My phone buzzed in my purse. I checked the text and read Jeff's name.

"Can we go home?" I turned to Seth and switched off my calls.

Melanie nodded. "They're releasing Margaret now. You can go back and tell her bye if you want."

I only made it halfway down the hall before beelining to the restroom and breaking down in tears.

Eight

PRESTON

I popped the top on a beer and took a long gulp before settling into the dark kitchen and dialing my mom. It was late, but I needed to hear her voice after my long day at the hospital. Being in that drafty place with all those miserable people had killed my vibes and put me into a funk. I could never be a doctor or some dude who helped the sick. The low energy that hung around healthcare places was depressing as fuck.

I always said the only doctor I could see myself becoming was a plastic surgeon for breast implants. I'd get to play with tits and make women happy at the same time. But performing life-saving surgeries with a side of possible death? No, thanks. I'd take my cushy office job over the hero complex any day.

"Hello?" my mom answered the phone in a groggy voice.

"Mom? Were you asleep?" I asked, checking behind me to make sure I was still alone.

Once we'd arrived back at the house, everyone had disappeared for an early night. But I couldn't sleep. I'd tossed and turned until I gave up and snuck to the fridge for a late-night buzz.

"Yeah, I drifted off," she said.

"Why? Are you feeling okay? Everything all right?" A trace of panic pulsed in my chest.

During her chemo treatments, she'd often tire so quickly that by dinnertime, she'd fall asleep at the table.

"It's nearly midnight, Preston! Of course I'm okay. What're you calling at this hour for? Are you okay?" She echoed panic back to me.

My dad grumbled in the background.

"I'm fine. Don't get yourself worked up. Sorry to call you so late. I just had a long day at the hospital with Margaret. I didn't want to tell you, but she's got breast cancer." I swallowed the lump that had formed in my throat.

"I know already, honey. I was one of the first people she reached out to."

"Why didn't you tell me?"

"Because you took my diagnosis so hard. I didn't think you needed to know unless things …" She lowered her voice and continued, "Unless things have gotten bad. Are they bad? Why were you at the hospital?"

"She reacted badly to the chemo, I guess. I don't know the details. I stayed as long as I could, but Seth and his girlfriend and Madison came up and took my mind off everything. But I didn't want to leave her, you know? Or Fred." I took another sip of beer, letting the bubbles tingle on my lips before swallowing.

"I know. You're as loyal as they come. Is she still there? How's Fred?" she asked.

"They're back home. Fred seemed okay, but I could see the worry in his eyes. Same look Dad wore. It's hard to watch, and it really sticks with me. It makes me question my future and life choices—which I don't want to do."

"Well, son, that's life. You can't go through it all willy-nilly. Things aren't always fun and games. You've had a perfect childhood, but that doesn't mean things will always be so easy. You can't control your future. Your dad and I might not be here tomorrow. You're not even guaranteed tomorrow. I wish I could promise you that your life would be all shits and giggles."

"Mom! You don't curse!" I nearly tipped my drink over, catching it before it fell over onto the counter.

She laughed. "I'm trying to lighten the mood. I don't like my son sad, and I hate that you had to see me at my worst. But I'm not going to blow smoke up your butt either. You questioning your life choices sounds promising, considering I know of your decision to live as a man-child forever."

"I never said I wanted to be a man-child!" I stuck my bottom lip out in a pout.

"You don't have to. If you don't grow up, that's exactly what you'll be. Is that the life choice you're questioning? You afraid you'll die lonely now that you've seen some hard truths?"

"There's this girl," I started.

My mom gasped on the other end of the line.

"Go on." Her voice wavered.

"I think she might be worth me thinking differently about my future. But I'm not sure. I never thought of her this way until I saw someone else with her. And I don't know if she feels the same about me. I could be reading her signals wrong." I held the phone between my shoulder and jaw while turning the bottle in my hand and peeling back the label.

"What're her signals?"

"She said she hates me," I mumbled.

She sucked in her breath and whistled. "Better find another one then. No means no. I taught you better than to bark up that tree, or go down that road, or whatever you kids call it these days."

"But I don't think she really hates me. I think we have a sort of rivalry going on between us, and I'm seeing her a bit different. I think I might tempt her to see me a bit different too. You know, give up the party frat-boy lifestyle and be more …" I rubbed my jaw, clueless as to what I needed to do to behave in a relationship.

"Be more attentive to her, loving, supportive, interested, kind, and all that jazz."

"Yeah, that."

"Remember how you stood by my side at the hospital? And how you stood by Margaret today? And how you've been loyal to Seth and been his best friend for years, even when you two fought over that one worthless twit of a girl in high school?" she asked.

"Yeah."

"Do that but with this girl. If she likes you, she'll let you know. But don't push her."

"I'll try," I said, pausing at the sound of footsteps on the roof.

"Good. Let me know how it goes. It's about time for you to settle. Sanchez can't live in a bachelor pad forever. He needs a mama."

"He's got the best grandmama. He doesn't need anything else."

"Fine. I need a daughter-in-law. I've had too much testosterone in my life, and I need a woman I can get my nails done with. Someone besides my dreadful mother-in-law!"

"I heard that," my dad groaned in the background.

"All right. I'll let you get back to sleep."

"Good night, dear. I love you." She yawned.

"Love you too."

I hung up the phone and tilted my head, listening again. A familiar scraping noise came from upstairs. I hadn't thought about Madison's hiding place in years. There had been a handful of times, as a teenager, when I'd step outside into the night and turn my head toward the roof, watching her stare into space and seemingly contemplate life. But knowing Madison, she'd escaped to the rooftop to escape from me—or as I'd seen her do a few times, smoke a joint.

I rubbed the back of my neck and sighed. She was probably upstairs, crying her eyes out over that douche canoe. And if there were two things I was good at, it was loyalty and support. Sure, I could be a dick. And I cycled through women like Madison cycled through clothes. But I knew an opportunity when I saw it. My dad, the successful businessman, had taught me that.

I turned off the kitchen lights and tiptoed upstairs. A wooden ladder leading into the attic hung from the ceiling. I hoisted myself up into the musty space and pushed the flashlight button on my phone. I held it up, scanning the area. A chilly draft blew past me from the open window at the far end of the room. I hopped over a pile of boxes and wound through a bunch of junk before crawling onto the rooftop.

"What the hell do you want?" Madison asked. She sat, hugging her knees to her chest.

"Thought you might be here," I said, scooting next to her, scraping my palms on the shingles.

"How did you know I was up here?" She wiped a hand across her face and sniffled.

"You think I don't notice your habits? We've spent almost our entire lives together and just about every summer here. I pick up on things."

"So, you know I come here to think?" She squinted her eyes and stared off into the distance.

"Or smoke a bowl."

She laughed. Her voice carried into the night, drowning out the steady chirp of crickets.

"Or sneak a drink too. It's a wonder that you didn't fall off this roof some nights." I looked down toward the front yard. The blanket of fog that had rolled in days ago was slowly lifting.

"Some nights, I wanted to jump off of it," she murmured.

I sighed and lay down on my back, staring up at the stars. There was only a sliver of the moon left in the sky. My mom had told me crescent moons were just a peek at God's smile. And if I ever needed that piece of comfort, to go out and watch the night sky. I never paid that piece of advice any attention until tonight.

"I know the feeling," I said.

"You? What do you have to worry about? You seem to always be in a good mood. You get everything you want, just like a spoiled trust-fund baby. Like me." She rubbed her palms over her eyes and lay down beside me.

"And yet here we are. I'm just as lost as you. And today scared the shit out of me. It reminded me of my mom's battle with cancer and that no matter how hard I try to ignore serious issues, I can't. We'll all leave this place one day. And what if it's me in the hospital? Hell, I only have your dumbass brother to take care of me! That'd be a disaster."

"Ha! Good luck getting him to do anything other than flirt with your nurse. You'd be better off dead," she said.

"See? I've got struggles. Even if I hide them with beer, babes, and bullshit." I twisted my arms under my head, propping myself up off the hard shingles.

"You know, sometimes, I think as crazy as Hailey and Dominick were just to pack up and go, I only tell myself they're crazy because I'm jealous. It sounds romantic and dreamy. Can you imagine running away and starting over? It's got to feel like shedding a second skin and reinventing yourself."

"Why would you want to reinvent yourself? You're Madison Sheffield. Fashion expert and socialite extraordinaire. Just because some douche came into your life and made you question it, it doesn't change you."

"But it does," she sighed.

"No. It doesn't change you at the core. But it's changed the way you think of yourself and life, just like my mom's diagnosis changed me. At least for a little while. I pushed it out of my mind until I was reminded again. Now, I'm back to square one. Don't be like me and forget. Use your life lessons to make progress, better yourself. Next time, you'll see warning flags with that type."

I looked at her out of the corner of my eye. She flung herself up onto her knees and stared at me.

"Where the hell is Preston, and what did you do with him?"

"I have no fucking clue where this is coming from. I impress myself. Maybe I should take notes for the next chick. Is it working?" I asked.

"Yeah, you're still in there." She shook her head and lay back down. "I don't know what's going on with me either. Maybe we're growing up. Jeff made me feel different. It was perfect until it wasn't. Like, I started to question myself. I didn't know which way was up or down. And I know I should be happy he's gone because he was an asshole. But then again, he wasn't. He could be charming. I don't know what I did to set him off. I need to figure myself out. I think I'm too much—and why I'm confessing this shit to my worst enemy, I'll never know. I guess I just don't have anyone to talk to anymore after Hailey left. I'm not close to anyone as much as I was to her. I'm desperate." She pressed her palms to her eyes and groaned.

I rolled over on my side and propped myself on my elbow, prying her fingers from her face. "Get it together! You didn't do anything to set him off. I knew who he was the second after I, um … fucked your ass. There was a change in him. I guess you could say it brought out his true colors."

"What do you mean?" Her perfectly arched brows drew together.

"Look, there're assholes, and then there're assholes. I'm an asshole. But I'm only, like, a level eight. I don't do any of the intentional asshole stuff. Mostly. But Jeff is a solid level-twelve asshole. He's controlling and manipulative, and he was gaslighting you. It's … abuse."

"What? No way. I would have noticed it. Besides, that shit doesn't happen to women like me. I don't tolerate it." She shooed me away.

I hesitated before slowly continuing, "But you did."

"No. I would have known if he'd knocked me around." She pursed her lips.

"He doesn't have to knock you around, Madison. I'm telling you, that dude was bad news. He tricked you."

"How do you know this? What the fuck is gaslighting?" She propped herself on her elbow, raising her gaze to my level.

"Because, like I said, I'm an asshole too. So, other assholes think they can speak asshole to me—and they can. But I have boundaries, whereas a lot of them don't. And I don't hide it. The evil ones do. Gaslighting is when someone manipulates you and makes you question your sanity. Sound familiar?"

A look of panic crept into her gaze before she quickly looked away.

"See, I know you're putting the pieces together. Just admit it. I'm not that kind of an asshole."

"Yeah, you are! You tried to let those poor chickens loose in the halls back at high school! You know they would've gotten trampled to death. That's an asshole move. Not to mention, the shit you've done to me throughout the years!" Her eyes snapped back to mine.

"Those chickens would have been fine! It was a harmless joke. I can't believe you brought that up. I was so mad at you when you ruined that prank. That would have been the most epic senior prank of all time." I sat up and tucked my legs under me. The rough shingles had already scraped my elbows and hands raw.

"Is that why you're so mean to me?" she asked. "Why you treat me so bad?"

"Huh? Do you really feel that way? I thought it was just fun and games between us. I knew there was this deep tension, but ... I kind of liked it. I thought you did too."

"And there it is." She pushed herself up, folding her long legs crisscross out in front of her.

"There what is?"

"That's why you're single. It's not because you're a bachelor for life. It's because you're terrible at reading signals," she said.

I put my hand to my chest and gasped. "Not me. I'm a ladies' man. I'm a bachelor for life because I choose to be."

"Bullshit. Do you think I like the crap you pull on me? You're out of your mind. It's infuriating and a turnoff." She rolled her eyes.

"You didn't seem turned off when we were doing the fuck-off." I pouted. This conversation wasn't going as planned. I'd been looking for the perfect, opportune time to tell Madison how I felt. But instead, I'd reverted back to asshole mode.

"The what?"

"The fuck-off. You fuck me. I fuck you. It's like a competition. You know ... the butt stuff we did," I said.

"Jeez. You're not helping your case any on how you aren't an asshole." Her nose wrinkled in disgust.

"No, I said I wasn't a level-twelve asshole," I corrected her. Again, another asshole move.

"Whatever. Besides, the fuck-off didn't count. We didn't actually fuck." The corners of her mouth twitched into a grin, as if she'd won our argument.

"Are you serious? Were you even there?"

"Of course I was there. But you only screwed my mouth and ass. It doesn't count. It's like what virgins do these days. Haven't you heard? As long as you aren't diving into my pussy, we haven't fucked."

"This is brand-new information." I rubbed my jawline, contemplating all the women that I hadn't fucked. This brought my numbers down substantially.

"Poor Preston. You can take my notch off your bedpost." She patted the top of my head.

My heart fell into my stomach. I had been proud of that notch. It was my most impressive notch to date. I'd thought I conquered her. Banging my best friend's sister was straight out of porn and something I liked to relive in my head more times than I'd admit. My shoulders slumped forward.

"It was a fun memory anyway. I didn't mean to hurt you then. I didn't, did I? Was it—was I—did you ... like it? Did you really mean that when you said you had better sex with a clown than me?"

She threw her head back and let out another laugh before answering, "You and your ego."

"I'm serious. How was it?" My pulse quickened.

I'd never stuck around long enough to prod my dates on how good "The P" was. I'd assumed I was a rock star in bed because they usually kept coming back. But when Madison had made the clown comment, I'd seriously started to question my previous flings' motives. I did own a giant bank account and harbor a network of connections that was the envy of all of my frat brothers.

"Fine—" she said through gritted teeth.

"Just fine?"

"You didn't let me finish."

"I was saying ... fine, I'll tell you."

My head bobbed up and down as I anxiously awaited whatever knife she was about to pierce into me.

She took a deep breath and winced. "I liked it. It felt good. You ... felt good. I don't know if maybe it was the sexual tension or the rough play or what." The words tumbled out of her mouth in a long and quick run-on sentence, as if she couldn't get the vile thoughts out of her head fast enough.

I stopped listening after she said she liked it. Before I could think, I pressed my lips to hers, but she pushed me off and dropped her jaw.

"Why did you do that?" she cried.

I wiped her cherry-flavored lip gloss from my lips and stared back at her in horror. "I have no idea. It just seemed right. Fuck. I'm sorry. Let's get back to hating and playing games. I don't like this feeling I'm getting right now anyway." I bit my lip, tasting her again.

"Me neither. Are you trying to take advantage of me in my desperate state of mind?" She pointed her finger at me, wagging it.

"Hell no, I'm not taking advantage of you. Remember, I'm a level eight!" I swallowed hard and tugged at my collar, mentally giving myself an ass-kicking for royally fucking up my romantic confession.

"Will you?" she whispered, dropping her lids and fumbling with a loose string on her blouse.

I rubbed my ears and tilted my head. "Sorry. I don't think I heard you right. What?" I craned my neck, straining to hear her.

"I said, will you?" she mumbled again.

"Will I what?" My pulse skyrocketed. I braced my palms against the roof to steady myself.

"Take advantage of me." She swiftly moved her face within inches of mine. Her breath tickled against my jaw.

My dick shot up, pitching a tent in my pants in response.

"For fuck's sake." I darted my eyes toward the window and back to her before answering, "How do you want it?"

Nine

MADISON

Who knew that a dose of depression would cause me to wiggle out of my panties like a pledging freshman at a Greek Row frat party?

Once I told Preston that I needed us to end this war right here and right now on the battlefield of my bed, he hopped to his feet and dragged me through the window. I landed on my heels atop the creaking attic floor, stumbling over into a stack of empty boxes.

"Shh. You're going to get us caught!" Preston reached for my hand, pulling me back up and into him.

I shot my hand out and curled my fingertips around his neck. His Adam's apple bobbed under my palm, and he took a deep gulp of air.

"I don't give a fuck. I like it raw and risqué." I licked my lips and groped his cock with my free hand.

He growled before prying my fingers from him and turning me around, pinning both of my wrists to my lower back and pushing me against the back wall. My cheek smashed against the dusty Sheetrock.

The firm bulge in his pants pressed into me as he whispered into my ear, "I'm going to fill that rude mouth of yours with my cum and make you choke it down if you keep talking like that."

I squirmed under his grasp, pushing my hips back into him. "I'm going to sit on your face and smother you until you can't breathe. You're going to die, drowning in my wet pussy."

"No better way to go." He sank to his knees.

He hooked his fingertips under the waist of my leggings and pulled them and my panties to my ankles. I flattened my palms to the wall and braced myself.

He spread me apart with his palms and dragged his tongue up my slit before turning me around and tucking himself under my pussy. He dug into me with an iron grip and forced my thighs open. His fingers teased me apart while he circled my clit with his tongue.

I arched my back, straining against his jaw while he pushed two fingers into me. I threaded my fingers through his thick hair and roughly pulled him into me.

"Fuck," I moaned, rocking back on his hand while fucking his face.

He drew his head back and gasped for breath, meeting my gaze. "You like that, don't you?" His tongue traced over his lips, slick with me.

"You think you can make me come?" I sneered, peering at him through my half-lidded eyes.

His fingers still worked inside me, picking up the pace.

"I know I can."

He swiftly pumped his arm up and down, burying his fingers inside me until his knuckles crashed hard against my pussy lips. His other palm pressed me hard against the wall. I struggled against his grip, but he kept shoving his fingers inside me repeatedly, all while holding me steady. He locked his eyes on mine and smirked that arrogant expression I'd come to hate.

I opened my mouth to let out an insult, but when a rush of hot liquid shot down my legs, I could only breathe a sigh of relief.

"What the fuck was that?" I asked, watching him lick his tongue straight up my wet thigh. My knees shook out from under me.

"That was just the beginning." He stood up and swept me off my feet, slinging me over his shoulder. He turned his head and bit hard into my ass cheek while I tried to catch my breath and make sense of what had just happened.

I'd never been touched like that before, much less had someone make me shoot out a questionable slippery liquid. But the knowledge that my body could perform new tricks turned me on more than my concern over the puddle I'd left in the attic.

I stayed speechless while he effortlessly carried me down. His muscled arms clung to my legs, securing me safely against him. I still felt a tiny trickle release from between my thighs with each bump and jostle down the ladder.

"You taste like a fucking snow cone. A warm one." He licked my hip and kicked open the door to my bedroom.

"Shh! Someone's going to hear us. And what the fuck? A snow cone?" I arched my back and straightened my body.

"I thought you weren't worried about anyone catching us?" He smacked my ass hard.

"I am when my bare ass is in the air!" I hissed, still pissed that he'd said I tasted like a snow cone.

Why couldn't he have said I tasted like a cupcake or heaven? Or something equally as romantic and suave? But then I remembered, I had just creamed on Preston Lancaster's face, and he wasn't exactly known for his romanticism.

"I can take care of that," he said, flinging me onto my back on the bed.

His fingers laced through my leggings and panties as he pulled them off and tossed my leggings to the side. He brought my panties to his face and sniffed them, drawing in a long breath. I sat up and spread my legs, eager to finally feel him inside me.

"I'm going to win this fuck-off. It's already one to zero," he said before wiggling out of his boxers. His erection sprang up, nearly knocking me on my chin.

"The hell you are," I growled, snatching up his boxers and bringing them to my face. I took a deep breath and swallowed the scent of clean laundry—thankfully.

No one, especially Preston, would out-fuck me. It was war he wanted, and it was war he was getting.

"I've never had a woman do that before. Fuck, that was hot," he said, pulling his shirt up over his head. He gripped his cock in his palm and stroked it while watching me. The deep ridges of his chest flexed with each pump of his hand.

"Get on the bed." I jerked my head toward the massive pile of pillows that I'd slept on earlier.

"I thought I was going to—"

"I said, get on the fucking bed." I clenched my teeth and tore my top off, slinging it over his head. My fingers fumbled against the clasp of my bra, unhooking it.

"Madison, you're … you're a fucking goddess." He openly studied me, raking his eyes from my collar to the lasered bare spot between my legs before lying down on the bed.

"Look who's winning now," I said, crawling atop him and leaning forward.

I reached toward the nightstand, brushing my stiff nipples against his cheeks. He caught one in his mouth and nibbled it between his teeth. I pulled a condom out of the drawer and tore it open.

"I give up. I don't want to win if this is the prize for losing," he mumbled into my breasts.

I flushed with an urgent need as I rose up and swung my body around. I straddled him backward and rolled the rubber onto his dick before slowly guiding him into me. His thickness wasn't for the faint of heart.

"You like that?" I moaned, leaning forward and gripping his knees with my hands.

I bounced on his cock while he watched, mesmerized. Reverse cowgirl was my signature move. It always returned the same results—making men putty in my hands.

"Fuck, baby. Keep going." He put his hands on my waist and slammed me into him harder.

The tip of him rammed into my cervix, causing me to wince with a pain that made me drip again. He brushed his palm over my ass before smacking it and stretching my cheeks apart. His thumb pressed into my asshole as he dribbled my hips like a fucking basketball. I hopped on his lap, gaining more momentum with each shallow moan of his.

"Fuck. I can't take it anymore," he groaned, gripping me around the waist again and lifting me off of him.

"So, I win?" I said between breaths.

"Hell no. It's my turn." He flipped me over and pushed me into the pillows.

"Oh, damn." My voice shook as he propped himself up on his fists and buried himself deep into me.

His legs tangled with mine, pinning my trembling thighs down into the mattress.

I curled the bedsheets into my palm and brought them to my lips, stifling my moans. I raised my hips and shoved my other hand down my stomach until I reached my clit. I twirled my fingers around my sweet spot until I felt that familiar building tension tingle throughout my lower body.

"Are you going to come for me?" he grunted, smacking his hips into my ass.

"Mmhmm. Don't stop," I said as he steadied his rhythm.

I lifted my head and turned toward him, locking my eyes on his and searching for his lips. I needed his tongue between my teeth while I bucked with wave after wave of pleasure. I couldn't find my release until he kissed me like he wanted me, not like he was doing me a favor.

"Kiss me," I whispered, dropping my gaze to his mouth.

His face softened as he brought his lips to mine and hungrily took my breath away.

I wiggled my fingers against my clit and let myself go over the edge, trembling underneath his rigid body while he tore his lips from mine and cried out in pleasure. He kept going, only collapsing beside me when my moans stopped. We took several minutes to catch our breath before one of us had the post-sex courage to speak up about what the hell had just happened.

"So, I guess I'm not winning." I tucked a pillow under my head and sighed.

But Preston didn't answer me. His eyes glazed over in thought as he gazed at the ceiling.

"I have to tell you something." He rose on his elbow and turned toward me.

"Shit. What is it? Do you have herpes? I didn't see lumps or bumps. But if that's the case, that is going too far in this war! I wouldn't ever jeopardize your health, Preston Lancaster!" I smacked his shoulder with the back of my hand.

"No. I don't have herpes! Damn. I—I—" he said, wiping a bead of sweat from his brow. "I won."

He let out a deep breath and fell back on the pile of pillows, raking his palms over his face.

"Fine. You won that round. But … you know this all ends tomorrow. I'm like Cinderella. Once tonight is over, the spell breaks, and it's back to normal shenanigans. We can't exactly keep having a secret rendezvous. We'll hate each other in the morning. So … I can still catch up to your score." I sat up on the bed and winked. My ridiculously high endurance was just another one of my special tricks.

"Aww. You just have to beat me, don't you? You ain't mad, are ya, Maddie?" he said before I promptly smacked him with a pillow and sat on his face.

I woke up before sunrise and slid off the bed as quietly as possible. Preston slept like a baby. His disheveled hair from our fuck-off marathon stuck out in all directions, framing his face like he'd gotten the shock of his life. I probably looked the same. But I didn't have time to bother with worrying about my appearance. I needed to get the hell out of this place before he woke. How could I face him the morning after our all-nighter?

I hadn't planned on banging my brother's best friend, but I wasn't exactly complaining about it either. I needed that bedroom battle like I needed a reality check. One big dickin', and Preston set me straight and back on my path to boss-babe badass. After our last session, I lay in bed with fashionable sketches of a new couture line of lingerie dancing through my head. I drifted off with an expanded business plan and not even a thought about my ex-asshole, Jeff. Without knowing it, last night, Preston had been my savior and my muse.

But he was still also my worst enemy, and that was why I tiptoed around the room, shamefully packing my things to escape the lake house before anyone else rolled out of bed. I quickly stuffed my bags, wrinkling my silken blouses and scuffing my leather boots. I didn't give a shit. I needed out.

Preston whimpered in his sleep before rolling over onto his side. The sheet slipped from his back, exposing his bare ass. I paused from stuffing my suitcase and giggled. I momentarily thought about the things I could do to his vulnerable state, like shoving a cream pie under him for when he rolled back over or sticking a white flag between his cheeks. But I didn't have either of those things, and I didn't dare wake him. It wouldn't be worth it for me to have to confront him face-to-face about what we had done. So, instead, I finished packing and snuck out the door, locking it behind me.

I stepped outside and made my way toward my car, taking a deep breath of fresh air. The fog had blown away, leaving a clear view of the emerald lake that stretched into the distance. Water lapped at the edges of the pier, drowning out the morning birdsong. I took one last look at the lake house and sighed before stowing my luggage and pulling away. The sun's peak rose just above the horizon, lighting my way back to Forks.

I pressed the dial button on my car display and told it to call Hailey. I knew she wouldn't be awake at this hour, especially in her time zone, which was several hours behind. But I needed my best friend. Without anyone to confide in this last year, I'd spiraled out of control. I mean, I'd dated a borderline sociopath fuckwad, and I'd fucked Preston "The P" Lancaster, for goodness' sake. I couldn't get any lower than that.

"I did what you did," I said as soon as Hailey picked up the phone.

"What? What'd I do?" Hailey breathed out a long sigh.

If anyone was used to my dramatics, it was my bestie.

"I ran away." I drummed my thumbs on the steering wheel while clenching my jaw. I knew admitting what I had done would be tough. But I had no idea how I'd verbalize the confusing chaos I'd been a part of these last few months.

"Where are you?" she asked. A hint of panic creeping into her voice.

"Going home."

"But I thought you ran away?"

"I did. From my second home. The lake house." I veered the car around a corner and exited onto the interstate, revving my engine.

Hailey sighed. "That doesn't count," she said.

"It does when you're running away from bad decisions. It doesn't matter where I'm coming from. Just where I'm going." I nodded to myself and focused on the road in front of me.

"Oh shit. That's some pretty deep talk for this early in the morning. What did you do?"

"Fucked Preston." I lowered the volume on my speakers, preparing myself for a verbal assault.

"Again? As in after that first threesome, which you still haven't given me the details on?" Hailey's voice rose into a piercing shrill.

"What's going on?" Dominick groaned in the background.

"Nothing. Go back to sleep," Hailey said, giving Dominick a loud, smacking kiss.

"Now, back to you," she whispered. "What the hell?"

I heard her rustling out of bed.

"Trust me. You don't want to know those dirty details of the first time," I said.

"Yes, I do."

"I'll need a lot of wine to recount that night."

"Go on," she urged.

"Ugh. So, I fucked him last night too. I broke up with Jeff, and—"

"You broke up with Jeff? Why would you do that?" she shrieked.

I could hear her footsteps stomping away from her bedroom.

"Because he was an asshole!" I shot back.

"I thought he was sweet and independent and understood you and you two had fireworks sex. What happened?"

"It was all fake. Once we spent more time together, I learned he was full of shit. He started to get controlling and weird, and I'm pretty sure he was talking to other women— or doing more than talking to them anyway."

"Wow, Madison. I'm so sorry. I had no idea." Her tone dropped.

"That's okay. I fucked Preston to get over it." I ran my slick palms over the leather steering wheel and braced myself for what was coming next.

"How did that even happen? I thought you hated him." She clinked what sounded like porcelain and glass in the background.

She needed coffee for this convo, and I needed a sedative.

"One thing led to another. He was … sweet." I bit my lip hard and tried to hold back the verbal diarrhea I was on the edge of spewing.

"Sweet? Are we speaking about the same Preston? Are you high? Hold on. I need to wake up. I think I'm still dreaming," she said. A steady stream of liquid sounded in the background, followed by a very loud sip and sigh. "Okay, start talking."

"Remember me telling you about Margaret, the woman who takes care of the lake house?"

"Uh-huh."

"Well, she has breast cancer. And Preston and I stayed with her at the hospital when she took a turn for the worse," I said.

Hailey gasped and choked on her coffee.

"She's okay! She's okay!" I assured her. "But I saw a much more sensitive side to him that I'd not seen before. And later that night, he found me sitting on the rooftop. I sometimes go up there to zone out and get away. But he came and consoled me. He made me feel not just better, but also good. He took my mind off Jeff. And then we fucked."

"Wow. Just like that? I'm not sure which part to believe less. That you fucked just like that or that Preston was a sweetheart," she said.

"Preston was definitely a sweetheart, and I totally asked him to take advantage of me in my vulnerable, pathetic state. And knowing Preston—"

"He jumped right on it. On you."

"Exactly." I pressed my lips together.

"Okay, that sounds right." She took another sip of coffee. "How was it?"

"Better than I could have imagined. Just as good with Jeff but different. It wasn't only physical. I guess because we've known each other for so long. It wasn't awkward or anything. It felt right, and it felt good. Like coming home after a long day at work. So, naturally, I'm running away because I can't have that shit."

"Naturally," she replied in a dry tone. "Most people would call that a good time and want to stick around. But instead, you run away to embark on a new life after dumping your crazy ex-boyfriend and fucking your archenemy, who might mean a little bit more to you than you thought. It sounds like your roof is on fire. So, now what? What're you going to do?"

"Let the motherfucker burn."

"Which one? Preston or Jeff?" she asked.

"My roof! My life. I'm burning it down and starting from scratch. Well, not really. Just getting rid of my preconceived notions of alpha males. The weird thing is, last night, after our fuck-off—"

"Fuck-off?"

"Yeah, fuck-off. Preston and I basically battled it out in bed. But anyway, after that, I had an epiphany of sorts. An entire new line of lingerie under Minx along with proper business plans for a launch came to me after we finished the deed." My lips parted into a wide grin.

"Post-nut clarity. Dominick gets that. I can't say I've been so lucky. The only thing that happens to me after an orgasm is the need to pee or sleep."

"It's not happened to me either. The last person on earth I thought would act as my muse was Preston. But here we are."

"There you are. I'm over here, away from the drama."

"I thrive in it. You know that." I flipped the sun visor down, blocking out the bright orange sun still hanging low in the sky.

"What do you need from me?"

"The support of my best friend if I decide to call you with my post-nut clarity confessions. I miss you, ya know." My voice trailed off into a pitiful sigh.

"I miss you too. The mountains could use a Madison."

"Ha! Good luck getting me in Podunk. But maybe, one day, I'll head your way."

"I hope so. Now, go back home and get to work. I want to see your sketches. Don't get tangled up in too much drama. Stay away from sexy, snaky assholes and don't fuck Preston again unless you're desperate. Or unless you actually like him. You know, you could try to go on a serious date with him. I bet—"

"Sorry!" I blew a garbled noise from between my lips. "Static! I'm losing you. Talk later!" I pressed the button on my car display and hung up the phone.

I rested back against the headrest and drove straight to Forks without stopping. I didn't want any breaks or any time to think. All I wanted was to return to life as I had known it. But Jeff's name flashed across my car display, rudely distracting me from daydreaming about my Minx empire— and maybe a little of last night. When I didn't answer, he called again.

After the twelfth time my phone rang, I swallowed back the tightness growing in my chest and pressed the Block button. My quick dive into a real relationship had ended in disaster, and I swore off level-twelve assholes for life. But who knew? After last night, I might be able to settle for a level eight.

Ten

PRESTON

It had been two days since the sunshine left my life. When I'd woken the morning Madison left without saying good-bye, I'd felt like a piece of me had died. Even Melanie and Seth commented on my misery. Of course, I lied to them and said I was constipated. And in a way, I kind of was. I was backed up and full of emotion that I couldn't let out, no matter how hard I tried. I was a playboy for life. Love hadn't touched me—until she did.

I swatted a fly away and pushed my heel into the ground, rocking the hammock. A gust of wind blew through my hair, tickling my face the same way she'd brushed against my cheeks when she squeezed my chin between her thighs. I closed my eyes and took a deep breath, remembering her sweet scent and her snow-cone flavor.

I could live the rest of my life, satisfied with only that one snow cone. But Madison was unattainable. Women like her didn't settle for douche bags like me. It would take a miracle for me to undo the shit I'd put her through. And besides, Seth would kill me.

I raised my head and glanced back toward the house. Melanie and Margaret were coming my way with an armload of food and blankets.

"Picnic time!" Melanie shouted.

I hopped out of the hammock, nearly somersaulting to the ground before catching my footing.

"Where're Fred and Seth? Let me help you!" I rushed toward them and grabbed two bowlfuls of food.

"It's just us three. Seth is inside, sleeping off a hangover. And Fred is working down the street today. So, you get to spend time with two girls at once." Melanie winked, stacking a large casserole dish on top of the hefty pile of bowls I was carrying.

"Let's put it down there, by the tree." Margaret motioned toward a shady spot near the water. The color had returned to her face, and she was walking with almost a skip in her step.

I grunted and followed behind them. "What's this for anyway? No one told me we were having a picnic," I said, setting the food on top of the spread blanket.

We sat down and made ourselves comfortable.

"Melanie and I made it for you. She said you were pitifully constipated. We got lots of fibrous veggies, so you'll feel better. Eat up!" Margaret pried the top off of a bowl of salad, a bowl of oats, a bowl of broccoli, and a bowl of cabbage. "And wash it down with prune juice!" Margaret shoved a bottle of purple liquid in my face.

I cringed and wiped a bead of sweat from my brow.

"What's wrong?" Melanie teased.

"Um …" I scratched the back of my head.

"Did you lie to me?" Melanie gasped. "Something is bothering you besides your bathroom habits. Come on. I'm a nurse. You can tell me anything."

Margaret raised her brows.

"Jeez. No, I'm not constipated. I'm just having … feelings." The word burned my throat. I had never admitted to having feelings in my life. But if I had to bare my soul instead of choke down a bowl of rotten vegetables, I'd do it. But just this once.

"Bingo," Margaret said, exchanging grins with Melanie.

"It's Madison, isn't it?" Melanie asked. Her smile stretched from ear to ear.

"How did you know that?" A rush of heat spread across my cheeks. I suddenly wished I'd gobbled down the salad bowl.

"It was written all over your face at the hospital. When you two came in to see me. You didn't pay me a lick of attention! Your eyes were on her." Margaret folded her arms and grinned.

"Does Seth know? He's going to kill me." I buried my head in my hands.

"Why? For crushing on his sister? It's not like you slept with her!" Melanie rolled her eyes.

I didn't answer.

"Preston!" Melanie shouted. "You didn't!"

"I did."

Margaret threw her head back and laughed. "I knew it! It was only a matter of time before you two figured out you were made for each other. All this crap, arguing and bullying, was only because you were striving for the other's attention. I could see it plain as day. Anyone who paid attention could!"

Melanie sucked in her breath and scooted in front of me. "Look at me. Do not tell Seth you banged his sister. But I have already run by the *what if you two fell in love* scenario to him once before."

"Really? What did he say?" I asked. My pulse quickened. I checked behind me to see if my bro was close.

"He said he couldn't think of a better match for his sister." She patted my shoulder.

"Well, no need to worry about that. It doesn't matter how I feel. She hates me." I stared at the lake behind them. The wind was blowing the surf hard against the rocky cliffs.

"She slept with you." Melanie turned her palms up and shrugged.

"So?" I said.

"So, I think you have an opportunity here," Margaret said.

My ears perked at the word *opportunity*. I blamed it on my inner businessman, who I'd ignored for way too long in favor of babes and booze.

"You think I have a chance?" I asked.

"We do. And that's the real reason we dragged you down here. We're going to help. Let's call it playing matchmaker and meddling in business we shouldn't. But hey! It's keeping my mind off chemo, so I'll guilt-trip you into that." Margaret's eyes crinkled into a conniving expression.

"Fine. I think this could work. But I do need your help." I tapped the bottom of my chin and looked up toward the sky. The wind pushed a cluster of bright, fluffy clouds overhead.

"Sure. Anything. What do you need?" Melanie asked, following my gaze up to the sky.

"Aha! A chicken." I pointed at the chicken-shaped cloud.

"Yep. That looks like a chicken," Melanie assured me. "But what do you need?"

"A chicken." I dropped my gaze back down to her.

"Like a roasted chicken? Fried?" Margaret asked.

"No. A whole chicken. Cluck-cluck, feathers, laying-eggs type chicken." I shoved my fists under my armpits and flapped my makeshift wings.

"Is this another prank? I'm not sure that's the way to go about snagging your girl." Melanie's bottom lip overturned into a pout.

"No, it's not a prank. It's an offering!" I held up my palms, claiming my innocence. If you could call it that.

I'd save the chickens—or at least one chicken—and show Madison that I had a big heart to match my big dick. And if she wanted, I could give her both.

I didn't know a damn thing about chickens, much less where to get one at the lake. But thankfully, Margaret and Fred had connections with the local farmers market and one famous farmer in particular. He'd sold prized poultry to state fairs for livestock competitions for decades. His chickens were sought out all over the South and usually fetched a handful of awards. A prized chicken would be the ultimate peace offering for Madison.

But unfortunately, with the way things were going, I did not receive a prized chicken. Instead, I'd shelled out two grand for a massive, molting beast named Henrietta. The farmer had handed her to me in a hurry, shooing me away because he had business to attend to. It wasn't until I reached the car that I understood how full of shit he was.

Once I let Henrietta down, she clucked the entire way back to Forks. She didn't just cluck like a regular chicken. This bird screeched, howled, and even grunted like a caveman before she popped out a pebble of an egg in my ride.

"Damn it, chicken!" I said to her reflection in the rearview mirror. "You've turned my ride into a barn!"

She shrieked and flapped her wings, sending a handful of feathers floating onto my leather seats.

"I'm warning you! You're supposed to win me the girl. That's why I bought you. You come from a line of prizewinners! Go figure that I end up with the only birdbrain on that farm." I rolled my eyes.

Henrietta let out a squawk and hopped onto the back of my headrest, perching atop my head.

"Fuck!" I swerved my car onto the side of the road and slammed on the brakes. "Get off! Get off!" I shouted, plucking my new feathered enemy out of my hair and setting her down beside me.

She cocked her head to the side and flew up, squatting to rest on the passenger headrest.

"What the cluck?" I pointed my finger at her. "You stay put. Try that move again, and I'll fry you up for Sunday supper."

Henrietta mumbled a long series of clucks, as if she were mocking me.

I drove the rest of the way to Greek Row with one eye on her and one on the road. By the time I reached the BAD sorority house, Henrietta had fallen asleep, still clinging to the passenger headrest.

"Cock-a-doodle-doo, butt nugget! Time to shine." I picked her up and tucked her fat ass under my armpit while hoisting us both out of the car.

The ordinarily chaotic street nearby campus was eerily quiet and empty. Most of the college students had left to return home for the summer.

I dragged my feet across the yard and rang the doorbell. The porch leading up to the BAD house was just as you'd expect a fashion academy porch to look. The front doors were painted pitch-black with a modern, styled window. A swag of fresh greenery clung to each gaslit sconce on either side of the double doors, and flowerpots full of flowers dotted the exterior. Henrietta squirmed in my hands.

"Fine. I'll let you down. But don't move!" I told her, setting her on the porch.

A younger sorority sister I'd never seen before answered the door. Her jet-black hair flowed down her shoulders, stopping just above her asymmetrical-cut neon crop top. A row of tight abs peeked from above the waistline of a low-slung skirt. If I didn't know she was a member of BAD because I was at their sorority, I would have known easily from the way she was dressed.

"Can I help you?" She looked past me from underneath a thick row of lashes and stared down at my chicken.

Henrietta stomped her feet across the stone porch, clucking in rhythm to her march.

"I'm looking for Madison." I tore my gaze from her body and tried to behave.

"She left. She doesn't live here anymore." The girl's eyes grew wide as Henrietta hopped down the stairs one by one and took off in a run across the lawn.

"Damn it!" I ran after the chicken, scooping her up into my arms and cradling her like a baby. "Where did she move to?" I shouted between breaths, walking backward back to my car.

"Some apartment in the city." She shrugged.

"Thanks." I turned to leave, stealing one last glance at the young girl.

"Weirdo." She shook her head and shut the door.

"Weirdo?" I said under my breath, tossing Henrietta into the car. "Fuck. I think I'm the creepy old man now. What's happened to me in the last month since I left this place?"

I looked in the mirror and tugged at my face, trying to find any clue or wrinkle that I'd suddenly aged. Henrietta squawked and settled back on her perch.

I dialed Seth's number on my car display before pulling away and heading into the heart of the city.

"What up, sister fucker?" Seth answered the phone.

"Uh, about that. I guess Melanie told you." I sucked in a long breath through my teeth and braced myself.

"All I know is that I had one hell of a hangover this morning. And I woke up, and you were gone. Melanie said something about you saving a chicken to offer my sister because you two got freaky. I don't know what the hell you're doing with that chicken, but that's clucked up."

An awkward silence filled my car.

"I'm afraid to ask if you're being funny or not," I said.

"Dude, I don't care. Go get my sister. She can handle herself. I'm not too worried about it. She's more likely to break you than you are her. But I don't want this to change our bromance."

"It won't. Maybe we'll be one of those couples where something like this brings us closer together."

"Yeah. Like having kids but not. Or like one of us cheated, and the other has forgiven the cardinal sin. I forgive you, Preston. For betraying me and banging my sister."

"Thanks, bro. Now, can you tell me where she is, so I can deliver the goods? The chicken … not 'The P.' Sorry. Too soon?"

"Gross, man. Just don't tell me about it. She's at the old apartment on Main. The one my mom used to rent out to that hot chick I fucked our freshman year."

"Excuse me?" Melanie's voice screamed in the background.

"Kidding! Kidding!" Seth said before quickly whispering, "Main Street, fifteenth floor. I know you remember that babe. She had a twin. And—"

"Seth!" Melanie shouted again.

"I got it. I got it. Thanks." I hung up the phone.

"Bawk-bawk, bitch! Time to do the damn thang!" I patted Henrietta's head and put my pedal to the metal.

The chicken looked at me and hissed.

Seth was right. I remembered the hot piece of ass he'd dated years ago. She was an exchange student from Australia, and everything about her was exotic. She spoke with a sultry accent, had skin the color of a vanilla latte, and wasn't a prude when it came to raunchy humor or sex talk. Her equally hot twin sister was supposed to come visit her over the summer. I texted with her back and forth and waited all year for that hook-up. But as my luck would have it, Seth's chick had left the States before the end of the semester, and we never heard from her or her sister again.

I drove the few miles to the Sheffield apartment in silence. My palms began to sweat again, and my stomach turned with anxiety.

What if Madison really hates me?

What if she kicks me out and bans me from ever talking to her again?

What if she hates Henrietta?

What if she laughs at me?

I swallowed hard. I'd only ever been rejected once, and that was by a legally blind chick. She read my personality, not my banging body, and ran the other way. Usually, women noticed this sweet face first and then fell for my charms. But not that date. She sat across from me for five minutes, told me no, and then left with her dog. I always wondered if the mutt had had something to do with it. Like maybe he had been trained to sniff out douche bags, and, well, I had been a douche bag back then.

I couldn't exactly call myself a jerk anymore. I'd saved a chicken from the slaughterhouse and driven all the way back home to deliver it to my childhood sweetheart. Even though Madison was anything but my childhood sweetheart. She was more like my childhood nightmare. One time, Madison had even signed my yearbook with a limp penis and my name on it. I slammed the book shut and offered to show her that my johnson wasn't anything like the pathetic pickle she had drawn in the annual. But she'd only pinched her two fingers together and laughed in my face, making me feel like a loser. She was the only one who could do that to me.

"*Ca-caw*," Henrietta called as I pulled to a stop in front of Madison's apartment building.

I grabbed my chicken and exited my ride before scurrying across the parking lot and into the building. Madison's apartment was the only one with a balcony, expanding the entire fifteenth floor. The priceless skyline view stretched for miles toward Outer Forks.

Most of the year, the apartment remained empty. I knew because Seth and I used to sneak over here to drink when we were underage. But on occasion, when Ms. Sheffield liked to entertain certain male guests away from her private residence, she stayed at the penthouse. Or at least, that was the word on the street. But who was I to judge a playgirl? Madison's mom lived my fantasy life, minus the string of ex-husbands.

I held Henrietta still with both of my hands while we got on the elevator. Once it started to move, she flapped her wings and squirted a mess down my entire pant leg.

"What the fuck? Are you afraid of heights? Sheesh! Now, I have to woo Madison while covered in chicken shit," I groaned, holding her at arm's length.

The elevator doors parted to her double-doored entry, where Jeff stood, knocking.

"Chicken shit, eh?" Jeff asked as I stepped from the elevator and out into the hall.

"What're you doing here?"

I skimmed over his designer suit, tailored to hug every curve of his muscles. The top two buttons of his button-up were unclasped, exposing his tree-stump, muscled neck. I glanced down at my chicken-shit-on pants and the feathers clinging to my shirt and stiffened.

"I could ask you the same thing." He smirked, eyeballing Henrietta.

Madison swung the door open and gaped at the two of us, plus one—a chicken.

"How did you two know I was here? And what the hell do you have a rooster for?" She folded her thin arms across her chest and stuck her hip out in a posh pose. Even pissed, she looked like a supermodel.

"It's a chicken, and her name is Henrietta. Gosh! Don't insult her like that!" I covered Henrietta's head—or where I thought she had ears—with my palm.

"I'm here to chat. I have no idea why he's here. I'm assuming some sort of juvenile prank." Jeff rolled his eyes.

"No, it's not a prank. I'm here to chat too." I took a step closer to the two of them while Henrietta ruffled her feathers.

"Too bad I'm not in the mood to chat. I've had enough of the both of you."

Her eyes fluttered to mine, and I could have sworn I saw a trace of lust flash across her. I knew because I'd seen that look with all the babes I knew. The hard-to-get game was strong. One minute, chicks refused me entry, and the next, they were begging for "The P."

"I only need a minute." Jeff inched closer to Madison.

"I can come back another time," I said, gluing my eyes to Jeff. I was prepared to leave, but he had to go first.

"I'm not up for it right now, Jeff. I've moved on, and we're not going to work out. So, anything you have to say will be pointless. I'm focusing on Minx—and myself." She pushed her hair back from her face and stared up at him.

"But I said I'm sorry. What more do you want from me?" He rose his voice and slammed his fists on the side of his hips.

"I think she wants you to go." I bristled.

Henrietta let out what sounded like a growl.

"I don't remember asking you." Jeff turned toward me and sneered.

His stupid, arrogant face flushed a bright red. I could practically see his blood pressure rising in the veins bulging in his forehead.

"Stop," Madison started but was interrupted by what I'd like to call the flying-chicken maneuver.

Henrietta flapped her wings and closed the distance between Jeff and me, landing atop his head and digging in with her claws.

"Get her off! Get her off!" Jeff screamed, running in circles and trying to pry Henrietta from his hair.

"Don't hurt her!" Madison yelled, reaching up to grab the chicken.

"I'll fry her in a bucket of grease if she doesn't get off!" Jeff swatted at his head, knocking the chicken loose.

She floated down, straight into Madison's arms, but not before leaving a pile of chicken shit tangled in Jeff's hair.

"You could have killed her, swinging your fists around like that! What if you'd knocked her out?" I yelled.

"You know what? This isn't worth it." Jeff stomped off toward the elevator and smashed his finger on the button. "You're not worth it." He looked at Madison and blew out a breath.

"Hey!" I swiveled on my heels, looking directly at him.

He seemed much smaller and less threatening with a pile of shit atop his fat head.

"Don't speak to her like that! She is worth it!" I turned back toward Madison. "You're worth it. That's why I'm here. That's why I came to chat. And that's why I saved the chicken. Or this chicken. Because you're worth it."

"For fuck's sake. What a joke." Jeff stepped into the elevator and flipped us off before the doors closed.

"Good riddance. You'll never have to see that jerk again."

She lifted her gaze to mine. "Do you really mean that?"

"I mean ... you can see him if you want, but I'm hoping you won't. He's an ass!"

"No. The other thing you said. You think I'm worth it?" she asked.

"Would I have driven all the way from the lake with an annoyingly massive beast of a chicken, just to show you how I feel?"

"Elaborate. I don't want to read too much or too little into this gesture. Are you telling me I'm a chickenshit?"

"No! Where would you even get that idea?" I touched my hand to my collar and winced.

She tilted her head at Henrietta, who lay, snoozing in her arms.

"I guess this signal is pretty hard to read." I twisted my mouth. "What I'm saying is, I like you. I might even be in love with you! I have no idea. I've never been in love before. But I think this is what it feels like. All those years I wasted, antagonizing you, was just me trying to get your attention in an extremely unhealthy way."

"Really? Well, I guess I can see that. I don't know what a healthy relationship looks like either. Obviously."

"Maybe that's something we can figure out together."

"Why now though? What happened to bring about this sudden realization that you've fallen for your brother's bratty little sister?"

"I think it was the night of our first fuck-off—when I ripped you a new one. Felt good." I shrugged.

"You're still the same. But I won't fault you for it. I can deal with a level-eight asshole. But I'm pretty needy, just so you know." She let out a long, dramatic sigh and stared down at her arms.

"I've grown up with you. Of course I know this," I assured her.

"Oh, I'm way needier now than ever before. I'm starting my own business, living on my own, and I lost my best friend." Her voice trailed off, a sniffle catching on that last admission.

"I can be your best friend." I reached out, curling my finger under her chin and lifting her gaze to mine.

She was the most beautiful thing I'd ever laid eyes on, and I'd laid eyes on a lot.

Henrietta let out a soft cluck.

"And Henrietta too," I added.

Madison set the sleepy beast on the floor and stepped closer. I circled my arms around her tiny waist, and she draped herself on me; it was like I was wearing the world's sexiest and most lavish suit, The Madison Sheffield.

"I can't believe we're doing this," she said, trailing her fingertips up my jawline.

"Doing what?" I smirked.

She pressed her lips to mine and mumbled into my mouth, "Winning."

Henrietta cooed at her heels.

Epilogue

MADISON
ONE YEAR LATER

Hailey held out her finger next to mine, taking a picture of our engagement rings and hashtagging *bride* before uploading it to social media.

Last year, we had been the socialites of Forks. This year, we had grown into our brands. Minx had taken off—as I'd planned, of course. Every ounce of blood, sweat, and tears I'd poured into my business was gaining traction at a speed I'd expected—not too fast and not too slow. I was on a steady up-and-up, on par with my bestie, who was becoming a dominant force in the fashion industry out west.

Hailey had a creative niche that I didn't have. She was vintage, and I was lux. We went together like orange juice and champagne or boots and fur.

"Do you ever regret leaving?" I asked.

"Nope," Hailey said. "Best decision I've ever made." She turned toward me. "Do you regret letting yourself fall in love?"

"Nope. Although it hasn't been easy—that's for damn sure. It's hard enough, taking care of myself, but now, I have to think of another person! Good thing I won't ever be a mom." I swatted a fly away and sighed.

"Still no kids, huh? I think I'd like a few running around. Dominick and I have talked about it. Course, he wants five."

"What? Do you have any idea what that would do to your waist? Things wouldn't fit you like they do now! You might as well forget those designer labels you love." I gasped.

Hailey clicked her tongue. "I don't care about that as much anymore! It wouldn't compare to having something Dominick and I made, cradled in my arms."

"Couldn't you make something less … needy? Like grow a houseplant and cradle it."

"I love you so much." She laughed.

I'd missed my best friend dearly. Preston had tried to fill the role she'd left, but he wasn't much into manicures and mimosas. But still, he tried. One morning, he'd even made brunch and burned it to a crisp. He scored an A for effort.

"Good. I know I'm difficult. Glad you can put up with me." I squeezed her arm and snuggled in closer to her, like the old times when we'd lain on the bed back at the BAD house and contemplated life in a not-so-sober state of mind.

"So … about my wedding. I know I asked you to be the maid of honor. But I think I want to say to hell with it and elope. It's all becoming too stressful for me," Hailey said, pushing us into a swing on the hammock.

A chilly wind blew off the water, whipping her pink curls across my face. I sputtered a piece of hair out of my mouth and acted like I was surprised by her confession.

"Really? You're going to run off again? You? Nah!" I teased.

She laughed and twisted her ring on her finger. "It's so much more romantic though!" she said.

"No way! Do you know what's romantic? Designing your own wedding dress and your fifteen bridesmaids dresses. And picking out crystal centerpieces. Oh, and creating bouquets! Don't forget the cake, the food, the seating arrangements, the invitations. I want it all, and I want it dipped in platinum." I held my ring back up, turning it this way and that to catch the light.

"I wouldn't expect anything less from you or Preston. Gosh, I still can't believe you two are getting married. It's so crazy!"

"Tell me about it. We keep each other on our toes. Never a dull moment with us. I guess that keeps it fresh enough for him to be happy. We definitely don't see ourselves ever becoming boring. Not with our personalities!" I set my foot on the ground below and stopped the hammock at the sound of footsteps approaching.

"It's almost time for lunch!" Margaret called. Her hair had begun to grow back in little tufts atop her head, and her cheeks had returned with the rounded plumpness I remembered from my childhood.

Preston and I traveled back to Cloverly as often as possible to be with her and Fred during treatments. We studied their healthy relationship, picking up on how to communicate and respond to each other, all the while being there for our friends in need.

Margaret had even helped me design a new line of fashionable hats to keep patients' heads warm. The launch was a success with all profits donated to breast cancer awareness and research. I'd enjoyed that side project just as much as I enjoyed Minx, and after my ridiculously large and lavish wedding, I planned on doing more charity projects like that. I'd heard a particular farmer needed a place for his oddball chickens, and, well, I had the funds and the friends.

Hailey had plenty of space to house a few chickens, but my new feather-child, Henrietta, was remaining with me.

"We're coming!" I shouted back to Margaret.

Hailey and I wiggled out of the hammock and made our way across the backyard. I glanced behind me to check for any signs of Preston, Dominick, and my brother. They had taken the boat out earlier with promises not to stop at any thot yachts. We'd eyed them suspiciously but agreed that we could use the break from their bromance.

I pushed open the door to the lake house to a very loud, "Surprise!"

A crowd of BAD sisters, my mother and other family members, Preston's family, and even Hailey's parents were gathered around us.

"What's this?" I turned toward Melanie, who stood, rubbing her growing belly.

"A surprise bridal shower for you two. Complete with a fashion show." She tugged my and Hailey's arms toward the living room, where a catwalk had been set up.

"Go on, sit," Margaret commanded while the other guests settled into their seats.

"Ready. Set. BAD girls for life!" Cheri squealed before pushing a button on her phone and sending music vibrating throughout our surround sound.

Preston, Dominick, and the rest of the DIK fraternity emerged from the hallway, modeling their veils and white dresses.

"Oh my gosh," I muttered, squeezing Hailey's hand.

She threw her head back and laughed when Preston lifted his gown to reveal a garter belt over a pair of white briefs. He gyrated onstage, twerked his butt, and blew me a kiss before letting Dominick take the stage in a fluffed-out princess dress. The freshman DIK members shifted on their heels and looked extremely uncomfortable.

"What're we going to do with these DIK-heads?" I shook my head, joining in on the laughter from the crowd.

"New rule for the BAD house. When they do shit like this, we marry 'em," Hailey said.

"Sounds like a plan," I replied.

THE END

Are you tired of the dramatic city life and ready to take on an adventure out west? Head to Buck Off Ranch and mingle with the cowboys in this brand-new small-town romcom series, coming soon.

Acknowledgments

As always, big thanks to my daughter, who keeps me going. Especially when I'm writing characters who make me want to pull my hair out.

Thanks to my amazing editor, Jovana, and my amazing cover designer, Lori. Also, Kim, my PA. I love my DTF team, and I couldn't do all this without them.

Thank you to the readers who have supported me on this journey and continue to encourage me to keep going. Your kindness has been a huge motivator in my life. I'm grateful for all of you.

And lastly, thank you to 2020 for filling me with the angst I needed to write this series. This is the last book I wrote in that hellacious year, and I have to say, *Good. Fucking. Riddance.*

To all the authors who have managed to continue writing during these hard times, providing the world with your art, entertainment, and beauty, you're all heroes.

About the Author

Kat Addams is a forever twenty-nine-year-old fashionista following her lifelong dream of writing contemporary romance inspired by the exotic men she meets in her worldly travels. At least, that's what she would like for you to think. She's certainly not a stay-at-home mom indulging in excessive daydreaming, frozen pizzas, an unhealthy addiction to purchasing pajamas, and one too many cocktails on the regular. That's some other romance author. The poor thing probably has to sneak away upstairs to write her dirty stories! What would her family think? Thankfully, that's not Kat!

Social Media:

Still crazy about Kat? Rawr! Stalk her on the social media platforms linked below!

https://linktr.ee/author_kat_addams

(For all of the links in one convenient location!)

Newsletter: https://kataddams.com/free-book

(Bonus *Hotty Toddy* Free E-Book)

Want to keep up with all the mischief and bad decisions? Be sure to subscribe to Kat's newsletter for the latest news. By becoming a subscriber, you'll be the first to know the juicy details on upcoming releases! You'll also be the first to hear of special offers, exclusive content, sneak peeks, terrible ideas, ridiculous shenanigans, and more! As a special gift for signing up, you'll also receive a free e-book, *Hotty Toddy*. Check below for more information on this stand-alone, second chance, and fake marriage novella.

Goodreads:
www.goodreads.com/author/show/19253462.Kat_Addams

Bookbub:
www.bookbub.com/profile/kat-addams

Amazon:
http://amazon.com/author/kataddams

DTF, Dirty. Tough. Females. (A Kat
Addams Reader Group):
https://www.facebook.com/groups/
DirtyToughFemales/

(A Facebook group to stay connected,
laugh, and share. Hope to see you there!)

Facebook:
www.facebook.com/KatAddamsAuthor

Instagram:
www.instagram.com/authorkataddams

Twitter:
https://twitter.com/KatAddamsAuthor

ARC Team:
https://docs.google.com/forms/u/2/d/e
/1FAIpQLScinoImFEIChW3PQ4_BrlBo
YxpcClYTftNZRz-1DmI-
121R8A/viewform?usp=send_form

(Interested in receiving Kat Addams's
latest books before release? Click the link
to join the ARC team!)

OTHER BOOKS BY KAT ADDAMS

DIRTY SOUTH SERIES

Hotty Toddy (Free for newsletter subscribers:
https://kataddams.com/free-book)
Grit and Grind
Nashvegas Nights
Mr. Big Ego
Mayday

DTF (DIRTY. TOUGH. FEMALE.) SERIES

On the Rox
Cream-Pied
Whip It Out
Just the Tip

FU (FORKS UNIVERSITY FASHION ACADEMY) SERIES

Sew Basic
Sew Haute

BUCK OFF RANCH SERIES

Josie Thatcher, Cowboy Catcher

**PARANORMAL ROMANTIC COMEDY,
WRITING AS FRITZI COX**

VILF SERIES

Ghosted
Royally Drained
Royally Cursed

FOR A COMPLETE LISTING OF KAT
ADDAMS'S BOOKS, VISIT
https://kataddams.com